Thorns of a Rose

I0676599

By

Sithabiso Sandra Ngwenya

Thorns of a Rose

Written and published by

Sithabiso Sandra Ngwenya
65 Hommer Street
Rustenburg North
Rustenburg, North West 0299
South Africa

Cell: +27740420499
ngilocy39@gmail.com

This book is a work of fiction. Any resemblance with any person, living or dead, is completely coincidental.

The cover photograph is courtesy
Retha Ferguson from Pexels.

ISBN: 978-0-62084199-3 Paperback

Sithabiso Sandra Ngwenya

Biography

Sithabiso Sandra Ngwenya (a.k.a. KittyKits Ngilocy) was born in December 1988 in Zimbabwe in the City Of Kings Bulawayo and bred in the small border town of Plumtree. She is a product of the acclaimed mission school Empandeni High School. She is a writer, poet, teacher and a soccer coach who finds solace in expressing herself through her writings. Currently, she is a student at the University of South Africa pursuing a Bachelor Degree in Education.

CHAPTER ONE

Lying between two monstrous mountains is the village of Umkhomo, which means the baobab, with its vegetation much more like the plumage of a vulture. It is the home of people with different cultural values; the most followed being the African tradition. Although there are Christians, theirs is the least number in the community. A small village school adorns the village square and a clutter of shops form what one would call the market place. It is a small community yet hosts a large number of occupants. A wide dusty road circles round the mountains and one can surely guess that it is the only road that leads to the huge towns. A cloud of dust swirls up from the road as an occasional bus or delivery truck passes through on its way to the city, carrying a bounty harvest of some farmer, leaving in its wake dusty villagers cursing at whomever is behind the wheel. Such is life of a small village, fashioned like a clock, always taking the same route but rather at a slow pace.

'Those peanuts won't shell themselves, young lady.' My mother's voice cut through my thoughts. Young lady! How I wish she would stop referring to me by that term. It made me feel so old, so grown up. A giggle behind me meant that even though mother had not meant for the entire world to hear, someone with sharp ears had heard what she said.

'Young lady, I bet you know what she means by that,' Aunt Nomsa chuckled as she sat down next to me and started shelling nuts. Aunt Nomsa, as I called her, was my father's sixth wife and the youngest. She was barely out of her teens yet here she was part of my father's train of

1

goods. I always wondered why she had agreed to such a life, to such a marriage. Why she had chosen to be part of this circus life she was leading? Yet, each time I tried to ask her, all she could say was she was happy.

'Not you too. I'm still a child and I just wish mother would see it that way,' I whispered back, shelling nuts vigorously.

'Thando, you're no longer a child. Those two pears protruding from your chest are not a curse, darling, and soon someone will be knocking on our doorstep asking for your hand in marriage'.

'Never! Father will never allow that. He promised me all the education under the stars and I know he would surely give me that,' I mumbled irritably.

'If you say so, my dear,' she said picking up her many skirts and disappearing into the kitchen.

Yes, I was my father's daughter and the only girl in the family. I boasted of sixteen brothers. When I was born, my father had named me Thandolwethu which means 'our love' and I was the only child who could wrap him around my finger and get away with it. My Grandmother always said it was a beautiful name with a deeper meaning, but to me it meant I was father's little girl, a princess, *intandokazi*.

Circumstances surrounding my birth have always remained a mystery to the family. My mother, who happened to be the first wife, had been married to my father for years and failed to conceive. That had led to my father, a massive traditionalist, to marry another wife. As if two wives were not enough, he married again and again and all his wives bore him children, but none bore a girl. This weighed heavily on him as he wanted a girl child who would make him a more respectable man in the society by increasing the number of cattle in his kraal when he married her off.

My mother suffered all vile insults. Women in the village drank tea over her name; she was called all sorts of names. She was sidelined from many rituals conducted for women all in the belief that she was cursed. My Grandmother would call her in *inyumba* each time she had had a calabash too many of the famous African beer. When all hope was lost, my mother fell pregnant and on the day I was born it was a full moon. Everyone saw it as a good omen. Father named me Thandolwethu because I had brought love back into the family. I had brought unity and more than ever, I had uplifted my mother's status in the community.

I finished shelling the nuts and took the basket to my mother who was busy nursing a huge fire to heat up the big enamel pot for the evening meal.

'Thank you, my child.'

She beamed as she took the basket from my hands. I nodded politely and sat right next to her, picking up the book I had discarded to do chores. Yes, that was me, the family bookworm. It was time to get lost in the land of white men.

CHAPTER TWO

'Aah! Yowee!'. A chilling scream broke through the silent night. I woke up with a start. Was I dreaming or what? A cold chill went down my spine as another blood curdling, agony filled scream disturbed the peace of the night. My ears felt as if they had the *Njelele* drum being played deep inside them. Groping blindly in the dark, I found the matches and lit the candle.

'Mother, Mother,' I whispered as my eyes got used to the dull glow of the candle light. No response. I went over to mother's sleeping mat, but it was empty. Where could she be, I wondered, my mind juggling all sorts of crazy thoughts. I hastily dressed and threw a blanket over my shoulders to ward off the chilly winter breeze. A huge fire was burning in front of Aunt Nomsa's hut. My heart skipped a beat. What could be wrong? Why were people gathered in front of her hut? I practically ran through the door, my foot missing the dish that contained various sterile tools by an inch.

'Mother! What is going on? Is she alright?' I asked in panic.

Okay, that is the dumbest question a seventeen-year-old would ask, for right before my eyes I could clearly see that Aunt Nomsa was in labour.

'I can't go on. I can't. Please make the pain stop', she panted like an old horse after a mini race. No one paid heed to her screams and pleas. Grandmother kept hitting her thighs apart with a stick as she tried fruitlessly to close them. My delicate sensibilities could not stomach it all. I heaved and like a rocket shot out of the house, my heels playing put-put with my buttocks. I shut the door of our hut behind me, my heart racing terribly. Oh my God! If giving birth is such an ordeal, I am not having any children, none at all.

The sound of loud ululating broke through the night accompanied by shrill whistles from the men grouped by the fire. The door creaked open and mother came through.

'Is it over, mother? Is aunt alright?' I asked anxiously.

'All is well, my child. You have a little sister now,' she said in a rather calm, emotionless voice.

'A little sister? Mother I have a little sister! *Nqayi! Nqayi!* My prayers have been answered. I'm a big sister now,' I chirped like a nightingale, hopping from one foot to the other happily.

The look on mother's face brought my joyful dance to a halt.

'Mother, what is wrong?' I asked with a concern-filled voice.

She was trembling slightly like a river reed after a storm and whenever she did that, it meant she was troubled.

'Nothing, my child. Come now and go to sleep. It's another long day tomorrow,' she said in her dismissive voice as she curled herself into a ball and threw the blanket over her head.

I was far too excited to sleep, but in the end I lost my battle with sleep and drifted off to dreamland.

Having a newborn in the family calls for massive celebration, but as the weeks went by, it soon began to get under my skin. Endless visitors came to our home all day long and I was the unfortunate one who suffered by preparing endless pots of tea. I wondered if all these people were there to congratulate aunt or just for a free cup of tea. In my books, congratulations should last for a week, but now it was almost two months since the birth and the path to our home had become clear as if some workmen had gone over it with a roller.

'Thando, here comes your great aunt and her husband. Can you please make another pot of tea?' mother called out to me.

'Mother, I'm tired. Why can't somebody else make the tea? I have school work to complete and I have been on my feet the whole day,' I said, pouting my lips.

'Now you listen to me *ngane yami* (*my child*). You are no longer the youngest child in the family and I don't want Buhle to pick up bad habits from you at this tender age,' Mother scolded in her authoritative voice that meant if I wasted a second trying to negotiate I would kiss the earth in seconds.

I bit back the retort that danced on tip of my tongue. Of late everything was about this baby. Buhle this, Buhle that, Buhle there; it was just so irritating. I no longer existed and this tiny, toothless baby had replaced me in everyone's hearts. I felt so stupid to be thrown from my throne by a baby. Dutifully, I did as told with a heavy heart. My only solace was the comfort of the school house. Little did I know that my paradise was soon to be taken away from me.

Elders say that before a huge storm comes by, accompanying showers tend to grace Mother Earth. It's the same with human nature. Before something massive goes down there are bound to be events that will throw teasers. I was lying half asleep under a mango tree on a hot, sunny day when I heard distinct voices murmuring. I strained my ears to catch what was being said, but all I heard were murmurs. The voices seemed to become clearer and now I could really hear that one was Aunt Nomsa's voice and the other belonged to Grandmother.

'How are we to break the news to her, mother?'

'Hmm. That will be a challenge, my child, considering how fragile she is.'

'But mother, isn't there any other away to sort this issue out. Don't you think we are being a little drastic by taking this step? Should we not try some other means of handling all this than this particular method?'

A worried edge sat on Aunt Nomsa's voice.

'What is to be sorted, aunt,' I asked walking up to them.

Yes, I startled them and the expressions on their faces were amusing.

'Thandolwethu! How many times have I told you that you should never eavesdrop nor interrupt adults when they are having a conversation?' Grandmother scolded.

'*Awu magriza* (*You really old woman*), you do know that it's only you who can give me all the village gossip and no one else,' I said teasingly, giving my Grandmother a wink.

We all laughed heartily, but I could see that theirs was fake laughter.

'So tell me what other way? What is going on and what where you worried about, aunt?'

'Nothing, Thando. It's just something you will not want to hear,' she said dropping her gaze from my penetrating brown eyes.

'Well, I do want to hear it. Please tell me, aunt, or I will start singing about what happened to Aunt Paulina's favourite pot.'

'You dare not or I might also tell on you to Grandmother,' she said and we burst out laughing.

That was the bond that I had with my father's youngest wife. Calling her 'aunt' was a formality and a show of respect; otherwise she was a friend to me.

'Your cousins are coming over, my child. That's what we were talking about.'

Grandmother's voice cut through our laughter.

'Which cousins, Gogo? I hope you don't mean those ones from the North,' I asked, hoping she meant other distant relatives.

'*Utshaye kahle ntombi yami* (*You are right, my girl*), I mean those ones,' she chuckled.

I was doomed. Have you ever had relatives that give you a headache from the minute they arrive until the day they leave? That was the situation between my cousins and me. They would visit, but never want to leave and I was always struck by the crossfire. Being the only one attending school, I would be tasked to tell stories round the evening fire and what stories would a bookworm like me really tell apart from the ones I read from the huge books in the school library. It was a task to modify Oliver Twist and turn it into folklore for them. Once, one cousin had to ask me to explain why Oliver was called Oliver and not by an African name. How would I know why he was named so? Having them around would mean all privileges that belonged to me would be shared. I would not have Father's last piece of meat or be excused from fetching water at the crack of dawn. That was my family and even though I hated having them around, they did bring vibes to our home and that's all that mattered.

I had been caught up in my many thoughts about my cousins so that I didn't catch the silent conversation that transpired between my Grandmother and aunt. These two were definitely not telling me everything, but I let it slide as I had more things to worry about concerning the coming visitors.

'I will get you some tea, Grandmother,' I said disappearing into the kitchen, leaving the two of them to continue their interrupted conversation.

CHAPTER THREE

Months went by and with time I began to enjoy the pleasures of having a 'live' doll to play with. Buhle turned out to be the most adorable baby. As soon as school was over at the mission house, I practically sped home to be with her. My mother, on the other hand, did not warm up to the baby and I always wondered why. Was mother jealous about Aunt Nomsa having a girl child too? Did she feel her position to be threatened by her? Only mother could answer my many questions, but I had grown to know that the topic was a "no go" area. Aunt Nomsa, instead of losing shape, seemed to glow more ravishingly beautiful each day, much to the envy of my father's other wives.

I was nearing Aunt Paulina's hut when I heard voices so I stopped to listen. Yes, you guessed right. I'm always at the wrong place at the right time.

'Look at her! She prances like a show horse, acting as if she is the queen bee,' Mama Thembi, who was my father's fifth wife, snorted like a wounded buffalo. She had always harboured a grudge against Aunt Nomsa because she had taken her place and had been father's favorite ever since.

'Why do you worry yourself, my sister? She is nothing compared to you and soon Dani (that's my father's name, short for Danisa) will be gracing your bed,' replied Aunt Paulina, who held second place in the line of wives and happened to be the most mean.

I always wondered what father had seen in her, but as the saying goes, men are the weirdest species on the face of the earth. Father must have seen something in her. These two were close and whenever they were together no good came out of it.

'You reckon he will?' she asked in a doubtful tone.

'Why not? Do you think the other wives match up to you? My dear, didn't I teach you well how to handle that old bull under the sheets? How to scourge his manhood and keep him coming for more,' Aunt Paulina said.

Alright, by now you really want me to stop eavesdropping, but I was just rooted to the same spot and it was difficult to move away. These two were chatting away unaware that they had an audience right behind their hut and my curious teenage mind loved gossip a lot. Eavesdropping was my middle name.

'Hehe. Don't make me laugh. The bull tires and blacks out right after having a dip in this honeypot,' Aunt Thembi chuckled.

Loud hoots of laughter accompanied by the clap of hands sounded. I couldn't believe my virgin ears. Well, not so much virgin anymore because I'd heard quite enough to break their virginity. As the African saying goes *Ilizwi alivikwa'* (*Words can't be dodged*). I just could not deprive them.

'My dear,' Aunt Paulina said in a rather serious tone.

'Yes, sister?'

'You have to claim your place. Some of us were in your position, but I held the seat of the favourite until you came around. Don't let a bitch-producing sow take your place. Can't you see we produce bulls and what do they give, huh?'

'Bitches,' Aunt Thembi said and more laughter broke out.

I couldn't believe my aunts could be this mean, but what came next never sat well with me.

'Look at that old cow, Mama Thando. First wife and all she could give was a single child. Not just a child, but a girl who has always overshadowed our sons. That was the reason I came and in a space of time I had vomited four strong bulls,' Aunt Paulina said with a voice full of hate.

'My, the old hag, always on a high horse. One child and she thinks she is the queen. Sometimes I wonder if she is our husband's child,' Aunt Thembi put in.

Loud laughter broke out and I could've sworn a dozen people were in the hut. Whenever these two sat to gossip and laugh, their laughter shook the cockroaches off the rafters.

Without waiting to hear more insults sent my mother's way, I announced my presence.

'Good day, aunts. Father is calling both of you to the family hut,' I said as I stood by the doorway.

Aunt Paulina gave a start and Aunt Thembi's eyes popped out like those of a goat down with constipation.

'Thandolwethu. How long have you been standing there?' she stammered.

I gave her my most cheesy Colgate smile before answering.

'Long enough to know that there are many cows in my father's kraal,' I said calmly as I turned to go.

'Hold on, young lady,' she said grabbing my wrist.

I tried to wrestle free, but her grip was tight.

'Is this what they teach you at that money-wasting, wretched mission school of yours? To disrespect your elders and backchat as if you are perched on top of a horse?'

I shook and hung my head in pretended shame to avoid a long tongue lashing. I felt a sharp pull on my ear before I was pushed out of the hut. I chuckled to myself as I ran towards the family hut. It was time to hear what father had to say.

Everyone sat silently in the huge family hut. All my father's wives and my brothers were present. I had Buhle on my lap and she was the only one not anxious about this meeting. She kept on blowing bubbles with her saliva, much to Aunt Paulina's annoyance. My father sat on the only huge arm chair, whilst my brothers occupied wooden stools. One could slice the silence with a knife, but everyone knew better than to hurry father when he was preparing his tobacco pipe. Finally, after what seemed like ages, he took a few long pulls, put it down and spoke.

'I called you all here because I have something important to tell you,' he said laying his pipe on the makeshift ashtray made out of an old zinc plate.

He scanned all of us with his beady eyes and when our eyes met, I noticed that the affectionate spark I had grown used to was gone. Instead of holding my gaze as he always did, he quickly averted his eyes and looked away. As per tradition, my mother being the eldest wife spoke up first.

'Thando's father, everyone is here and we are ready to hear what you have to say,' she said calmly.

Aunt Paulina gave a tiny cough and wore a frown on her already ugly face. It killed her that everyone addressed father as Thando's father, but not by her son's name. Not that it mattered to my brother Dumisani, who adored me as much as I adored him. He always thought my being the only girl was special, but try telling that to his mother. It would be another story.

Father cleared his throat and spoke:

'All of you know that the harvest we had was not as good as we had expected and due to lack of rain our maize and tobacco crop did not survive. Hence, we have met up with some sort of financial crisis. The many tonnes of tobacco we sent to the factory were rejected as they did not meet the grade standard. Only a few were sold. All our hard work was in vain.'

Silence descended all around the room. Even baby Buhle's chatter quietened down as if she understood what father had just said. It felt as though a huge, dark cloud had engulfed us within its depths.

'Surely it can't be that bad, can it, father?' I asked, breaking the menacing silence.

It was my nature and all my brothers had grown to accept the fact that I never followed the theory that children do not speak before adults do.

'My dear, it is bad, very bad.'

'But father, you can handle it, can't you? You can find a way out of this situation as always?' I asked anxiously.

Everyone was silent and they had their eyes fixed on me. I felt a cold chill run down my spine. Why was everyone looking at me in such a weird way?

'Thandolwethu, my rose.'

'Yes, father,' I answered in a rather queer voice.

'You are the family's only hope,' he said in a trembling voice.

Before I could ask what he meant, a shadow fell over the doorway.

I froze.

CHAPTER FOUR

I was floating on a fluffy cloud, not your typical fluffy cloud with Cupid perched on it, bow and arrow in hand, clad in diapers ready to shoot at the hearts of young lovers. No! This cloud was dark, filled with all the horrors of a nightmare. If this was a nightmare, then it was a very bad one and I could not wait to wake up from it and return to the land of the living and be father's little girl.

My father, my protector, but...

'Thandolwethu, did you hear a single word I have said to you?'

Father's voice cut through my subconscious like a sharp knife. Pop went the weasel! The cloud broke and I found myself in the family hut, now empty except for father, mother and the one person I had grown up hearing stories about. They were the kind of stories that send chills of fear down your spine, yet to a child they brought curiosity that wouldn't have killed a cat.

'No, father, I won't do it,' I screamed the minute my throat got wet enough to let my rather squeaky voice out.

'But my child, this is the only way that you could save the farm,' mother said.

I shot her a look that was more deadly than Medusa's stare. How could she even open the slits below her nose and say such a thing to me, her own daughter, I wondered.

'Mother, I won't do it and that's final,' I screamed, pulling my most fierce face.

16

It seemed to have no effect on anyone because they did not show any emotion towards my wailing.

'My child, the situation is bad and there is nothing that your father has not tried to do,' mother said calmly.

I turned to father, but he averted his gaze from me. Fixing teary eyes on the bald patch on top of his head, I willed him to look at me, but in vain. Shifting my attention to the cloaked figure that now occupied one of the wooden stools, I addressed him.

'What business do you have here? What is it that you want from my family, from my father?' I spat like an irritated cobra.

A wicked smile danced on his crooked lips and I felt my blood boil. Was this monster mocking me in my own home?

'Now Thando, that's not the way to talk to elders,' mother scolded.

Without any word he stood up to leave. When he reached the doorway, he paused and said 'I expect an answer by the end of the week, Mr. Kulube.'

Then, he was swallowed by the darkness that had begun to gather. I sat dumbfounded like the gnomes in the mission gardens. I could not believe my family, especially father, had chosen me to give my life away and everything that I hoped to achieve in the name of saving the family. How can a parent do this to their own child?

A pat on my hunched shoulder gave me a stir.

'Lwethu?'

I lifted my head from in-between my knees to stare into the teary eyes of Aunt Nomsa.

17

'Come with me, my dear,' she said as she took my hand.

Without a word, I stood up and left mother and father alone. Silently Aunt Nomsa led me to her hut and half-closed the door before she forced me to sit on her sleeping mat.

'What am I doing here? Are you the one sent to convince me to agree to this absurd arrangement between your husband and bloody Abiyosa?'

'Calm down, my dear,' she said feeding more firewood to the glowing embers. After a few blows, the fire flickered and cast ghostly shadows on the walls. I sat like a zombie waiting to listen to her mumbo jumbo.

'Lwethu, you know when I first arrived here, you were the only one who was there for me, who accepted me and made me feel welcome.'

'And so you think that's supposed to make me feel better? Everyone was there for you. You had come for your husband and so my being kind to you had nothing to do with my situation. So stop trying to act as if you care with what happens to me. After all, I'm not your daughter,' I fumed.

'Your anger is understandable, my dear, and you are right. Everyone was there for me, but instead of you treating me like your father's wife, you gave me friendship and sisterhood.'

'Hehe. *nansi ingulube inginonela*! (*Are you kidding me?*) Sisterhood? Where is your sisterhood now, aunt? Sisterhood is warning me that this was to happen; sisterhood is standing with me. No! I believe what lies beneath your husband's animal skin is worth more than sisterhood.'

18

'Thando! Don't ever talk about your father like that,' she said, shaking me violently. 'If not for this family do it for your father, the one who loves you a lot.'

'But why? Why did father get himself involved in this kind of debt?' I asked, choking on the torrents of tears that were rolling down my cheeks. It did not make any sense that the family had such massive financial problems. Father had always been the pillar and the mastermind of all finances and it just amazed me how he had gotten himself tangled in this web and on the Devil's hit list.

Oh! You are probably wondering what I am on about. Well, let me enlighten you.

Due to the difficult harvest people had experienced over the years, father had kept the family afloat on borrowed money. This he had done by getting loans from one of the most notorious loan sharks, a man named Mr. Abiyosa. No one knew where he came from and why he decided to settle in some village that was a thousand miles from ours. Rumour had it that he was from up north, from far off native lands and he was a banished old chief. Some said he was just a rich old man who used and took advantage of the poor. To children, he was the monster in stories that we grew up fearing. Over the years, father's debt had become so huge that it had become hard for him to pay it back. Nature was also not on his side as harvests kept getting worse year after year. Now it was time to pay him back and father had nothing but me.

'So, Lwethu, are you going to do it?'

'No, aunt. I can't give up my life just because the family thinks it's the right thing to do.'

'I cannot say I understand because I can see how torn apart you are.'

'It's not fair, not at all. This is my life. Why me?' I sobbed bitterly

'Nothing is fair in this life, dear. I thought life was unfair too at one point.'

'But for how long, aunt? How long should I be gone?'

'Long enough to pay the debt,' said a voice I knew too well from the door.

We turned to find Aunt Paulina standing hands akimbo like a plucked peacock, a satisfied grin on her face. She came into the room and towered over us like Goliath.

'If it's a lecture you're here for, please spare us, Paulina,' Aunt Nomsa said in a tone I barely recognised.

'Oh, shut up, bitch-bearer. I'm here to talk sense into this spoilt brat.'

It took all my will power not to slap my father's wife across the face and take out all my frustrations on her.

'Hey, princess, days of being in this place are over and it's time to prove that you are your father's daughter. Like it or not, I will personally make sure that you go with Abiyosa. It's not like you have anything to do in this family.'

'What do you mean by go with him,' I asked, puzzled.

'Oops! Your favourite aunt hasn't told you yet? *Nci, nci, nci*, poor child, even those who claim to love you are hiding things from you. Let me break it down for you. You are no longer returning to the mission school because your father is broke and in debt. To pay it off, you have to go and work in the Abiyosa household so as to save the family's reputation and your father's dignity,' she said triumphantly, as she turned and banged the door shut behind her.

I turned to Aunt Nomsa and she nodded, tears rolling down her cheeks. My worst fear was confirmed. I was sold, but little did I know this was just the beginning.

CHAPTER FIVE

The weeks that followed Aunt Paulina's revelation on what awaited me turned to be the hardest and toughest of my life. Sleep became a thing of the past. Every night I cried myself to sleep. I became withdrawn from everything that I had interest in and worst of all I couldn't even face my parents. As for Aunt Nomsa, all I saw was betrayal. How could she, of all people, hide such a huge thing from me? How could she, who was like a big sister to me, let me build castles in the air and not warn me about the strong wind currents?

Yes, father had taken to a loan shark to keep the family afloat during difficult times, but I felt that that had nothing to do with me. Was it my fault that I had dreams, that I wanted to be a better person and live a life of no struggle, get away from our mountain-cooped village and explore lands beyond?

I had a dozen brothers that could have worked out this debt in the Abiyosa plantations, but no, that sly fox had to choose the one thing that my father loved the most, me. It's not that my many brothers could not do house work. Actually they did it better than I could, yet they were spared the gallows. I was bound to be the sacrificial offering.

'Is it safe to come in,' mother called from the doorway of her hut.

'You're already here so you might as well. After all, it's your hut,' I said rudely.

'Young lady, I can still use the rod on you as fast as a bullet. Who do you think you are talking to in that tone? Hee! This child!'

'You can do as you please, mother. It matters not to me. I'm already done for,' I whined, tears starting to roll down my cheeks.

If there was something that turned my mother's heart from stone cold to cushion soft it was tears. She hated to see me cry and this time around she knew how much pain I was going through.

'My dear child, don't cry like this. Don't torture your mother with your tears. Father did what he thought was best for the family at the time to keep the family from starvation.'

'What about my... my educa...tion? Wh...what about the life you always wanted for me and my dreams being fulfilled? Father promised; he promised, mother,' I sobbed uncontrollably.

'Many girls your age are married and have children. It was a matter of time, my child.'

'A matter of what, Mother? I want to study, get out of this place and be the pride of this family. Look at Mellisa. She is going to the big city to study at a very much bigger school. They call it a university. I want to follow in her footsteps, mother.'

'Oh really! Are you forgetting that this Mellisa of yours is not only from a filthy rich family, but also she is a white person? I see this school of yours has really made you delusional.'

Ouch! That cut through to my bone marrow like Shaka Zulu's assegai. They say truth hurts, but this was way beyond pain. It dawned on me that even my mother was in for this ruthless idea. I was determined to fight them, fight for my own right to choose and make my own decisions.

It was late one evening while I was busy lamenting on my many misfortunes that I was summoned to father's sleeping hut. I had made sure that I avoided meeting father ever since Abiyosa's visit. I had steered away from having anything to do with him such that I didn't know when he came and when he left. My relationship with my father had turned from sweet to bitter and I didn't care much. I dragged my body towards father's hut, weary at heart, but ready to oppose whatever he had to say. As I entered the dimly lit hut I readily noticed the musky smell of freshly picked tobacco leaves. If this old man didn't die naturally, tobacco was going to be his cause of death. He smoked like a steam engine. I squinted my eyes at the hunched figure that lay on the grass mat. After weeks of not seeing my father, I had not known that he had taken ill. Instead of the strong man I knew him to be, he had been reduced to a shrivelled wimp.

'Father?' I called out softly.

'My child, come here,' replied a frail voice that sounded more like that of a frog trapped in the Kalahari desert.

That was father and he had taken ill ever since I refused to be the family scapegoat. I bet that's what my Grandmother means when she says when elders stress a lot they get high-high. That's what was exactly eating up father. I sat beside him on the mat and held his shaking hand.

'Lwethu *ntandokazi yami*, (*my favourite,*) you are my only hope and my first heiress. I know your father is asking you to break an arm and leg for the family, but please can you reconsider before I am degraded more than I already am,' father said squeezing my hand tightly. He heaved and broke into violent bouts of coughs. I readily fetched a gourd of water and let him take tiny sips one at a time.

'Father, why?. You know the life I want. Not this way. Not with Abiyosa.'

'It's only for a while, my child. Then you can come back home.'

I didn't sleep that night. The image of father's frail body haunted me. By the time I fell asleep, it was already breaking dawn.

Was I dreaming or was someone kicking my bottom? I wondered. Opening my sleepy eyes, I made out a shadowy figure standing over me. Even if I were taking my last breath, I would never mistake the body of the dragon lady, Aunt Paulina.

'If it's not you shouting at me, you disturb my sleep. Ugh! *Umuntu asuze sikhathi bani*,' (*What time does a person get?*) I said in an irritated tone.

'Evil brat, get up! You are really a piece of work. Why can't you be gone already,' she said kicking me again.

'I'm warning you, aunt. Do that again I will forget you are my father's wife.'

This woman just had the nerve.

'While you are still sleeping like a pregnant snake, your father has been taken to Shadiku the healer and I entirely blame you. He... '

I didn't wait to hear what she had to say. Like a comet, I shot out of the hut, half-dressed, my heart guiding my legs towards the river where the healer's home was located.

Thorns of a Rose

I hoped I was not too late...

CHAPTER SIX

'Stay back! You cannot charge in here like a possessed rhino,' Opikishu, who was the healer Shadiku's helping hand, barked as he pulled me back from entering the sacred healing hut.

'I want to see my father. *Baba! Baba ka Thando,*' I shouted trying to break free from his grasp.

I felt my body being engulfed by warm arms. I turned and found myself in mother's embrace.

'Be still, my child. Calm down. Your father will be fine; he will get better. I trust in the healer,' she purred like a contented cat after a sweet bowl of milk.

That voice filled with love, that soft purr I had been deprived of for many days on end, seemed to work its magic on me and I allowed her to lead me to the side of the hut and we sat down. Wild thoughts were dancing *gwaragwara* in my head. It was all my fault, a soft yet strong menacing small voice kept on ringing. Just as Aunt Paulina had said, all that was happening was my fault. The loan father had taken was to put me through school, to see that I had all that other girls at the mission school had. His sudden illness was due to my hot-headedness. Everything bad befalling our family at the moment was just merely my fault. I felt as though I was the curse that had come clothed in joy for our family. If I had not been born or had been born a boy, I wouldn't have had to put father in debt. All that was happening was on me, only me.

Mother seemed to read my mind for she cuddled me even closer and said 'None of this is your fault, my child. I've always told your father to lay low on his tobacco pipe and his amarula wine, but you know how adamant he can be. You are both cut from the same cloth, stubborn and pig-headed.'

I wish I could have said that those words made me feel better, but they made everything worse. Did mother really think that I was such a fool to believe her sugar-coated words? Hee! This woman! If father were on death's door and I was the reason for that, then I wouldn't be able to live with myself.

I held on to mother, sniffling like a lost puppy. The cloaked figure of Shadiku appeared in the doorway. Both mother and I went on our knees and bowed our heads in respect of the healer.

'*Mama* Thando,' Shadiku croaked.

'How is my father? Is he okay? Is he awake? Tell me please, oh messenger of the gods.'

I sprang up from my knees like a jack-in-the-box, aiming for the door. The humble old man stepped aside to let us in. The dimly lit hut did not give much light, but I could make out the traumatising sight that checked me. The once alpha male of the village, the envy of all men in the village, the one who sent women's hearts racing, had been reduced to a frail shrimp. Father's skin had wrinkled so much that he looked like an over-dried piece of biltong. He had suddenly turned from a vibrant man to an old timer. This is what I had done to my father. My stubbornness had reduced this man to a child. I had failed to see how bad the situation was.

'Can I be left alone with my father, please,' I asked quietly.

'Oh, so you can finish him off, you little ungrateful witch,' Aunt Paulina said as she shadowed the doorway.

Damn! This woman was just like leprosy, stuck and pasted in my life with invisible glue. What in the name of goodness had my father seen in such a monster?

'Not now, aunt, or maybe I should do something about you before I can give my father attention,' I spat out at her.

'Hee. Good people, do you see what I deal with all the time. This spoilt child has no respect for her elders', she cooed like a pregnant dove.

'Enough! Paulina get out before I curse you with the most worst curse under the stars,' Shadiku the healer hissed, half-dragging her out of the hut.

It wasn't easy for the frail healer to do so as Paulina was kicking and shouting vile insults at mother like a dueling wizard. Father started coughing, drawing in his breathe harshly.

'Please stop. Please,' he said wearily.

'Father, I am so sorry. All this is my fault,' I said kneeling beside him, mopping his sweaty forehead with my skirt.

'My child, it is well', he gasped.

I had not meant to drive him to this state, yet I could not stomach the thought of him lying helpless on that mat. It was decision time.

'Go well, my child. Remember it's only for a few months,' mother said as she gave me a tight hug.

I held on to her tightly as a baby kangaroo would. So this was it; I was the sacrificial lamb. I was paying for the sins of my father. I gathered my bundles of clothes and loaded them into the donkey cart. I avoided eye contact because I knew if I did look at them, I would break down completely.

'Finally something good has come out of you. Good riddance to bad rubbish,' Aunt Paulina whispered in my ear.

I shot her with eyes full of hatred, but I bit the words dancing on the tip of my tongue.

'Travel well, my dear. I know it is hard to give up your dreams. All will be well,' Aunt Nomsa said as tears rolled down her cheeks.

Yes, she was not just my father's youngest wife, but she was more of a sister to me. I said my teary farewells to everyone and then climbed aboard the donkey cart which was to take me on a two-day journey to the Abiyosa plantations. My elder brother had offered to take me to my so-called new home. Slowly the cart left my home, the mules sliding slowly like a hearse. It was as if they sensed the sadness in the air. My heart burst with pain as I watched my family being left behind.

'Wait!'

A voice broke through the solemn silence.

I half-stood in the donkey cart to see over the gathered heads, trying to figure out who had shouted. I saw a slight figure running towards the cart. It was someone I knew very well.

'Brother, stop,' I said jumping from the moving cart. I ran towards the cloaked figure that had suddenly broken from the mini crowd I was leaving behind. It was Louisa, my white friend from the mission school.

'Please don't go, Thando. Please don't go. I will talk to my father. Please don't leave. Don't leave me all alone, my friend,' she cried, hugging me tightly.

'Lou! What are you doing here?' I asked, tears rolling down my cheeks creating massive stains on the white blouse I was wearing.

'I can help you, my friend, help you get away from all this. You need not do this.'

I wished it were easy for me to take this offer from my dear friend, but as much as I wanted to take the offer, I loved my family more. I loved my parents more.

'Take care of them for me, Lou,' I said, boarding the cart again.

'You too, my friend,' she said squeezing a bulky envelope in my hand. I looked into her blue eyes and she nodded.

'This will come in handy in times of need, only in an emergency,' she said as she was left behind by the moving cart.

The journey began.

CHAPTER SEVEN

A long journey it was. We travelled through rough plains, rocky mountains and dense bush. On the day I left home, all I could do was cry silently. My brother tried to soothe the pain I felt, but in vain. As night engulfed us, we sought lodgings at a homestead that was by the road. It was not that I needed any sleep, but my poor brother was weary from manning the cart for long hours on end. My eyes were swollen and red like a baboon's bum from all the crying. My body was stiff as if every fiber in it had been frozen. I was slowly having second thoughts about the decision I had taken. Part of me knew that I had no choice, yet another opposed the decision I had hastily taken.

The homestead we had come upon belonged to an elderly couple who seemed to be nice people. They offered us warm water to bathe and food, yet the old lady's eyes never seemed to leave me alone. As I was about to undress so I could curl up on the sleeping mat next to hers, she pulled me by the hand.

'Turn around, my child,' she said softly.

Shocked at what she meant, I did as she requested and I felt her boney hands move up and down my back.

'Oh, Great Shango, what have you brought to my doorstep?' she exclaimed.

'What do you mean, Gogo?' I asked, fear creeping in every part of my body.

'You are a very special child, yet your path is filled with darkness, doom and sadness. You are an incarnate of the gods.'

'Gogo, I don't understand.'

'There is no need to understand. When the time is right, all will be clear to you,' she said, covering herself with a blanket.

Wild thoughts ran through my mind. What did this old lady mean? Why had she scrutinised my naked back like an archaeologist going through dead bones? Yes, I was born with a queer birthmark on my back, but my parents had never said anything about it and neither had my own Grandmother. Sleep came the hard way, but eventually I drifted off in troubled sleep.

Morning came and we bade the kind, elderly couple farewell. I couldn't shake off the feeling that Gogo's penetrating stare gave me. She had really shaken me up, but I couldn't bother much because so much lay before me. Down rocky plains we urged the donkeys pulling the cart, trying to set a pace so that we would reach our destination in record time. Conversation between my brother and me kept decreasing as we neared our destination. My brother could barely look me in the eye and I could barely do so myself.

'Thandolwethu, my beloved, I'm sorry. I can't keep this to myself anymore. Unfair as it is, there's something that I have to tell you,' he said, breaking the silence.

Oh Lord, what now? I wondered my heart skipping a beat as I fixed my eyes on him.

He cleared his throat before he sadly answered me.

'I know that you were told that you are to stay in the Abiyosa plantation for a couple of months or a year, working to pay off father's debt.'

'Yes, I know and the minute I pay off the damned debt I will rush back home,' I said firmly.

The stare he gave me before he could continue spoke volumes.

'My sister, you are never coming back home.'

'What do you mean?'

'Thando, for someone intelligent you are surely dumb. I overheard father and mother talking. Due to the debt, father agreed to marry you off to Abiyosa. That way the debt would be paid and it will unite the two families.'

Words failed me. My heart felt as if it was being ripped from my chest. The pain I felt was massive.

'*Mtaka baba*, please don't cry like this. As your elder brother, I just had no choice but to follow orders to drop you off at the Abiyosa plantation.'

'Please... *ngiyacela yazi lami... (I beg of you, brother)* can we please go back. Don't send me to my death. Rather you go and leave me with the elderly couple we met and tell father you left me at the plantation.'

I wailed like a young widow robbed of her love by death. I stood up ready to jump off the moving cart.

'Thando, stop it! I have no choice. Do you think that I want to do this to you? Do you think I want to give away my beloved sister?' he asked, pulling me back down and setting the donkeys on a wild run. I fell on the mat and let the river of tears flow.

I don't know how long I sat with my head between my legs, tears creating pools on the cart floor. After what seemed like ages, I felt the cart slow down until it came to a halt. I raised my head slowly like a gecko stalking an unsuspecting fly.

'This is where I leave you, my sister,' he said as he jumped off the cart and started to unload my few bags. I sat rooted to the cart, my body numb from the pain I felt from within.

'Come dear, I believe that truck on the hill is the one to take you to your plantation,' he said, helping me down from the cart.

For the first time I took note of my surroundings. We were parked at a huge gate. The land that stretched from the gate was so vast that I mistook it for a village, yet it was land belonging to one man. The gigantic gate looked more like hell's gates to me. I wondered how a sane human being could erect such a huge gate to house a farm. I bet the devil is a show off, I thought.

'Thando, I've to go now. I've fulfilled my task,' my brother said, as the truck came to a halt in front of the gates. Slowly the gate creaked open and I felt as if I was entering hell itself.

'Thandolwethu, be strong. I hate what the family did, but I have no say or power to oppose it,' he said holding me close in his arms.

A fresh stream of tears began to flow, but he wiped them off with his shirt. Turning to the stranger who stood watching us as if we were crazy, I silently nodded. He loaded my bags in the truck and opened the door for me. I climbed aboard and he shut the door firmly. I couldn't bear to look back; no, it was too much. As the truck covered ground and separated me from my brother, I couldn't hold it anymore. I turned back to catch a glimpse of him. His back was turned and he was urging the donkeys on like a madman. Deep down in my heart, I knew he was hurting inside.

With a deep sigh, I sat back and faced the life that awaited me in the Abiyosa plantation.

CHAPTER EIGHT

Down the gravel road the truck roared, distancing me from my brother. Even though I could no longer see him through the rear view mirror and the clouds of dust, in my mind I could vividly see his huge frame driving the donkeys on. The man behind the wheel did not utter a word nor even spare me a glance, but kept his eyes fixed on the road. Within a short space of time, the truck came to a halt in front of a huge, white-washed house, which was flanked by many thatched huts. The white-washed house was built the same way that the mission house was built, the only difference being that this one was bigger and it was thatched. All these structures screamed "prison" to me and I was to be in their confinement for God knows how long. Their sight brought nausea up my throat, but who could blame me? No one.

'Young lady, you may get out now.'

The driver's voice cut through my mind. Reluctantly, I alighted from the truck and followed him to one of the huts that had its door ajar as if it was ready to gobble me up. A girl almost my age stood by the door, silently beckoning to me with her hand that I should follow her. Dragging my feet and the one bag I had managed to pry from the driver's clutch, I followed her into the hut. The bag was the only link between me and the world I had left behind.

'Welcome to the Abiyosa compound,' she said, speaking for the first time.

I raised my head that had been cast downwards and looked towards her voice. The sight that met my eyes could have halted the roar of a mountain lion.

I was standing in a huge hut, far much bigger than the mission school house back home. If I had been in my right frame of mind, I would have been wowed by this marvel. Its walls were adorned with the most beautiful woven African quilts and the floor graced different coloured mats. There was a huge frame which housed the picture of what looked like a scene by the river drinking hole.

'You will catch flies if you keep that mouth of yours wide open like that,' a much older voice said beside me.

I jumped and almost fell in shock as I came face-to-face with an elderly woman. She looked slightly older than the Gogo we had met on the way and her eyes shone of kindness.

'I'm sorry. I did not mean to stare at your walls,' I said, shame creeping up my face.

Gently she took my hand and led me to the far end of the hut where a heavily embroidered mat was laid. Looking at it closely I could make out a face from the many patterns in it. It was the face of Abiyosa. Oh my! This rich, stinky bastard even had mats with his face on them. Why did he want me to be his payment when already he had all the riches under the stars?

'If there is anything you need, just inform me,' the woman who introduced herself as Yemanja said, flashing me a smile.

'Well, there is nothing I need unless if you know a secret way to get out of this place,' I said, pouting my lips and fixing her with my "don't-you-dare" look.

'Where would the queen want to go? I'm sure I can take you there with no trouble. Just say the word,' she said, flashing me a smile.

'Really? You will? Please take me away from here; take me back to my parents,' I said, hope creeping back into my heart.

She gave a sarcastic laugh and walked out of the hut, closing the door behind her.

Damn! Stupid witch! She was mocking me and I had been so desperate I didn't even notice. I threw myself on the floor in frustration. I hated this place and everything that came with it. Even though my muscles were screaming for a real sleeping mat, I made up my mind that I was not going to sleep nor eat a morsel of food. They had put me in this room and I was not going to move an inch.

The door reopened and the young girl I had met earlier came in bearing a huge bathing basin. She left the room and came back with a bucket of water and a tray that was laden with plates filled with mouth-watering food.

'Please wash up and then have your food,' she said quietly.

'I'm not hungry and neither do I need your kindness. Please leave me alone,' I said, choking back my tears.

'You need to eat and clean up. You had a long journey and you need ample rest.'

'What do you care? Did they send you to come and torment me? Just go away and leave me alone, please,' I shouted.

'Hey, behaving like an over-priced peacock won't help you in this place. Yoo! Shoot me for trying to help,' she said, turning to go.

'If this food is so important, why don't you eat it yourself?'

'Hmm. I see. They always come in feisty like wild horses, but in the end they turn into submissive puppies and eat out of the master's hand,' she said, shutting the door behind her.

Scanning the room quickly, I looked for something I could throw at the already closed door, but found nothing apart from the tray that held the two covered plates. Oh my God! *Waze wangilinga* (*I'm being tempted*). The aroma tickled my taste buds and my stomach rumbled like a volcano ready to erupt. I stood and walked towards one of the windows. Drawing the blinds back a little, I watched the sun that was slowly getting lower. If I had been home, mother would have been preparing the evening meal, Buhle chattering gibberish as she sat on my lap.

Food! The thought of it seemed to draw me magnetically to the tray. I knew this was a fight I was not going to win. I grabbed the plate and began to gobble up the soft porridge and the thick gravy laden with chunks of meat. You would have sworn I was a poor street urchin. In a space of few minutes I had cleaned both plates.

'You were famished, isnt? Don't worry, I won't tell about your eating habits.'

'So are you going to sneak up on me every time?' I asked the girl who had brought me the food.

She chuckled softly.

'No, not at all. I'm Sidi by the way. That old lady you met, Yemanja, is my aunt.'

'I am Thandolwethu, but everyone calls me Thando.'

'That's a nice name. I like it,' she said flashing me a smile.

My heart melted. How could there be a sweet person in this hell hole. I had a feeling that Sidi and I were going to get along.

'I brought you a basket of fruit in case you feel hungry during the night.

'Thank you so much. You are so kind,' I said taking it from her.

'Now, please take a bath before your water gets cold and rest. We will talk tomorrow,' she said, closing the door behind her.

I gave a heavy sigh as I undressed and soaked my weary, bruised and tired body with warm water. After the much desired bath, I lay on the mat juggling many thoughts about how in a flash my life had turned upside down. I gave a heavy sigh followed by a long yawn. Lady sleep was slowly knocking and I just could not keep her out for long. I gladly drifted into a dead stupor. Although I didn't hear it or wake up, the door creaked open and a hooded figure entered the hut. Sleeping beauty had an audience.

CHAPTER NINE

I was sitting by the fireplace, roasting a maize cob. I could see him further off coming my way. I tried to run towards him, but could not gain much ground to close the distance between us. I wondered why he was so near yet so far. I called out to him a thousand times, but all he kept doing was beckoning to me that I should follow him. I broke into a run that soon turned into a sprint, but it was all in vain. Suddenly he stopped with his back still towards me. I put my entire strength into a final sprint to reach him. I laid my hand on his shoulder and brought him around to face me. Our eyes met and I stared deeply into the face of horror.

'Wake up! Stop screaming,' a distant voice broke into my dream. Someone was shaking me violently. I opened my sleepy, tear-filled eyes and stared into the eyes of a girl I knew, yet did not know.

'He was here! Right in front of me,' I screamed, sweat dripping from my forehead like dew drops on a misty morning.

'Who was here? What are you blabbering about? If you don't stop screaming you will wake everyone up,' Sidi said, mopping up my forehead and trying to clamp her hand over my mouth.

'My brother, he was here, but when I reached out to him he turned and he became someone else,' I sobbed.

'You mean he turned into your soon-to-be husband,' she said in a soft tone.

I looked at her and nodded silently. I was no longer lying in the same room or on a mere grass mat. I was now on a soft mattress in a much smaller hut and someone had taken the liberty to tuck me in. Weirdly, I was no longer wearing my own clothes.

'Who put me in this hut and why am I wearing these ridiculously clothes,' I said, tugging them vigorously.

Sidi chuckled heartily.

'Are you telling me that you have never seen a night dress in your life? Hee, village girls.'

'Say that again I will show you what a village girl is,' I snapped.

'Ehh, that was just a joke. You are just so stiff and tense early morning. The master of the house instructed that you should be dressed in that last night,' she said.

'You mean, … he… did he…' I stammered covering myself with my hands.

I even went to the point of checking if my vagina was still there. That made Sidi laugh hysterically.

'No, silly. I was the one who dressed you up and no one was here. It was only me. You surely sleep like a hibernating bear.'

Phew! The thought of that horrible monster seeing me naked was a hard pill to swallow.

Sidi brought a basin of water. My body was sore from the long journey yet the cold water felt like heaven on my skin. I scrubbed myself down not minding the audience I had from Sidi. Good Lord, this girl was such a real chatterbox that I forgot my worries for a moment. I found myself laughing along with her. In a short space of time, she told me almost half the village gossip, who to watch out for, and which old women were known as witches.

'...and there is Nanakongololo. When you meet her along the path, please turn around and go the other way, my dear. She is a very powerful witch. Heh! The things she has done, eh!' she said, clapping her hands.

'What has she done, Sidi?' I asked, while putting on my best Sunday dress.

Mother had packed all my best clothes so that I had no choice but to wear them. If I had been home, I would not have worn them just to roam around the yard and do chores, but in this place my good clothes looked like those of a pauper. Even the clothes Sidi was wearing were what I would call classy and neat.

My question seemed to open up a huge can of worms because the bulletin that poured out of her about how this so-called woman had mutilated people was fit for a news broadcast. Her banter was accompanied by hand gestures and facial expressions such that it was as though I was watching a play. We didn't hear the door open nor did we hear it close.

'So this is where you are,' Yemanja's voice brought us back to earth amid our laughter.

We froze and I almost choked on my tongue.

'No, no, great aunt. I was just attending to the chores that you assigned to me,' Sidi said in a trembling voice.

Was I missing something between these two?

'Hmm. I see you think that my great niece is here to be your servant. You have been keeping her here all this time while I had to roam the whole compound like a headless chicken looking for her, huh?'

I didn't know why this old woman was shouting at me in this manner, but I was not going to let her scold Sidi for something she didn't do nor shout at me as if she was my mother.

'Sidi is nobody's slave here. She brought me water and food. At least she does not mock me like some other people that I know,' I said.

It infuriated me a lot that she would just barge in the hut and start shouting.

'A newly hatched chick, yet you are already quacking like a broody hen,' she said, looking down at me.

I refused to be stared down by an old hag who was not even my mother.

'Sidi is here to help me so if you don't mind, please excuse us, Gogo. I don't care if I arrived yesterday, but you are not to talk to her or to me this way. Please leave right now!'

I almost screamed at her.

She reminded me so much of Aunt Paulina and the way she talked to us, it was as if I was looking at an older version of her. Thinking of Aunt Paulina made my blood boil. She had not only abused me, but had delighted in making my life miserable. The old lady left the room mumbling harshly about how uncultured I was and how bad an upbringing I had had.

'I wouldn't have said all that if I were you. You just dug yourself into a deep hole,' Sidi said sadly as she left the room.

Oh me and my big mouth. Why couldn't I learn to keep silent? I wondered as I cleared the plates on the floor, putting them by a corner. I threw myself on the mattress.

Enemy number one had been made.

Yemanja was really an older Aunt Paulina. She didn't even give me time to breathe. Early every morning she would barge into the hut and bang two tin pots right over my head to wake me up. I wondered why she could not just wake me up the way any other normal person would. My days seemed to get harder and harder as they went by.

'Why do I have to wake up so early morning each and every day just to do nothing?' I confronted her one early morning when she came to wake me up.

'Young woman, this is not your father's house. You do as I say or face the music,' she said in a snarly voice.

'What music, old lady? Do you think I came here by choice? Do you think you can do as you please with me? Wait until I get away from here. I will surely make you pay. I know powerful white people at the mission house,' I shot back at her.

She looked at me with her dark, hollow eyes and broke into hysterical laughter. Her laugh was the most irritating thing about her. Was she Aunt Paulina's mother, I wondered.

'Powerful white people? The nerve! You think your wretched priests who keep on feeding you stories about a man who walked on water can do anything to us? Young woman, it's high time you accept that you are here to stay and get rid of that fairy tale of yours. Now get your lazy bottom up and go to the grinding stone,' she said banging the tin pots in my face.

Ugh! I felt the urge to pounce on her like a deranged leopard and rip her to pieces. Who in their right mind would send someone to the grinding stone at the crack of dawn? And to do what? Just sit on the so-called stone on my naked bum until the sun was up. I really did not understand why they made me do all these funny weird things and try as I might to get Sidi to tell, she would just avoid the topic.

One sunny afternoon as I sat in what I had dubbed "my prison", Sidi came rushing in. She had that gossip look on her face that I had grown to love, but today I was not going to let her blab like a canary. I was determined to get some information from her.

'Before you say anything, Sidi, look at this,' I said, flashing my shiny bracelet under her nose.

Her eyes lit up like those of a pirate who has just discovered a treasure island.

'I will give you this if you tell me what I want to know,' I said.

She gave me a look of utter disappointment.

'Thando, do you think you can bribe me with that? Isn't that a reminder of your friendship with Lou? So how can I take something that is of so much value to you?'

'I thought maybe if I paid you, then you will tell me what I want to know. Why is it that I don't do any jobs? Why is it that I am made to do all these ridiculous things? Is this how I am to pay my father's debt?'

'There was no need to offer a bribe. I was waiting for the right time. I wanted to be sure that you can be a trusted person before I tell you,' she said quietly.

She cleared her throat before she spoke again.

'All this is to prepare you for womanhood. You have to do all this so that they may pass you as eligible for womanhood. It is the custom of this place.'

'But I never asked to be prepared for womanhood, isnt? I swear that old cow is responsible for this.'

'Hey, be careful of what you say. I've been in so much trouble because of you. I really don't want to be punished for your crimes,' she said laughingly.

Yes, she was right. I had been drowning her in trouble ever since the day I had arrived. Not that I wanted to, but those were the perils of being around a rebellious person like me.

One day I had mixed Yemanja's snuff with chilli powder. I know you may think that this was a bad thing to do, but that old woman had slapped me hard for refusing to be checked for 'velvet cake ears' that were long enough. I was not going to allow an old hag poke me in the disguise of being a gynecologist. Oh boy! The way she had run around the compound like a possessed person, screaming that her nose was on fire was a sight worth watching. I couldn't help but laugh my lungs out, but I had got punishment after that.

She had ordered that Sidi and I should not be given any food, only water, for almost a week and we had to sleep in the barn. Poor woman! She thought she was being severe, but didn't know that sending us to stay out in the barn was a mistake on her part. Under the cover of darkness I taught Sidi how easy it was to milk a goat. Growing up in the company of my brothers, picking a lock was easy and making vicious dog putty in your hands was even easier. We would sneak out to the kraal and have our fill from the goat's udders every night. Every morning Yemanja wondered why we were energetic for people who were being deprived of food. After a while she had let us free and poor Sidi was given such a lashing that I felt badly for always dragging her into my mess.

'Thando, you do know that sooner or later, things are going to change,' she asked quietly.

'I wish things could stay as they are, Sidi. I don't want to even think about what is going to happen. I was brought up here, yet I spend my days being watched like a hawk. Why won't they get to whatever I am here to do so that this uncertainty can fade away,' I said giving a huge sigh.

They say a person should be careful of what they wish for. It didn't take long for my so-called wish to actually start coming true.

CHAPTER TEN

Hours turned to days and days into weeks that spilled over to a month. Time seemed to move so slowly in this weird place. I settled into the new life that had been sprung on me forcefully. I was terribly homesick, yet I knew that seeing any of my family was more like an elephant's dream to have a petite body like an impala. Sidi became my solace. She kept me going even though Yemanja made it her goal to make me feel as miserable as can be. Until now I had not come into contact with the one who owned the plantation, not that it mattered, but it made me dread what my fate was to be. I was beginning to think that maybe I was to work off the debt since now Yemanja gave me more meaningful chores to do.

'Thando, hurry up. I hate arriving at the river at sunset,' Sidi said as she stood, legs akimbo, like an army commander.

'Sidi, Sidi, Sidi, you do know it's the best time of the day to actually fetch water. I mean, the boys will be returning from the veld and it gives you time to scout for one to melt your heart,' I said teasingly, pushing her.

'Shh! If the dragon lady hears you say that, we will be sent to the caves this time round not to the barn. Ehh! Thando, you are just too much,' she said, poking me in the ribs.

Buckets in hand, we laughed our way towards the river. Sidi had become more like a sister to me. She helped me in every situation, not to mention being my partner in crime. Amid bursts of laughter we followed the dusty narrow path that led to the river. This had become our daily routine.

Not that I really had to fetch water, but it was a perfect excuse to be away from Yemanja's sharp tongue and all that spelt the Abiyosa household.

I still had not figured out why all of a sudden everyone in the plantation had begun to treat me more nicely. Was it because they felt pity for me or they were hiding something? You couldn't really tell about these people and even if Sidi knew what was going on, she was definitely not letting on.

On our way we passed a group of teenage boys who made funny cat calls at us and we giggled as any other girl would. It felt so good to be out and see friendly faces that did not know about my plight and struggles. We got to the river in record time and, by Jove, found it unpleasantly packed. I had always avoided people of the area in fear of being asked a lot of questions I could not answer. I had had incidents whereby some village girls had taunted me to tears and if it wasn't for my right hand girl, Sidi, I would have blown off and beaten the hell out of them. I was a girl from Umkhomo and I wasn't about to let the people of this village forget that. I could have looked weak, but when it came to *intonga*, (stick fight) I was just as good as a herdboy.

'This time around, please pretend that they are not there. I know how they can be a pain in the butt,' Sidi whispered as we reached the river bank.

I looked at her and smiled. This girl really did not know me very well. I, Thando, to keep quiet? Never!

'Oops! Move over women, let the bride to be get fresh water for her old fox,' a chubby girl named Shaki said, pushing everyone aside and creating a path for us to get to the watering hole. Shaki, the village belle, the one considered to be the most beautiful and sought-after girl, was one of my least favourite people. She was a loudmouth and was very cheeky. Once or twice I had had a confrontation with her and, trust me, it always ended up badly.

'Cut it out, Shaki and let Thando be. Do you want her to repeat what she did to you last time,' Sidi spat out at her.

'She was lucky, Sidi. I let her win because of that old pig that you bow down to. If only she wasn't staying at Abiyosa's place, I would have crushed her,' she said harshly.

'Crush who? *Nci...nci...nci uyambona loba uyankhanyisa?*' (Are you undermining me?) I said, taking a step towards her.

'Hey, don't come here with your clicking tongue. I don't understand what you are saying. *Nimbaya (Ugly person)*!'

'Don't bother yourself with old maids, Thando. That's all they know what to do,' Sidi said, pulling me away.

'Old maid, did you say? At least I don't have to carry the weight of an old goat on these ripe melons of mine,' she said, shaking her humongous breasts in my face.

Gosh! This girl was carrying mountains on her chest. Hoots of laughter broke out amongst her friends and they broke into song.

Ya bikira, Ya jamala, Bali chakula ili mbweha,

'*Thando, Thando, Thando.*

Ya bikira, Ya jamala, Bali chakula ili mbweha,

Heeh! Heeh!

(The virgin, once a beauty, now food for the old fox.)

I felt my blood boil to a point that I would have seared anyone's skin just by touching them. These imbeciles were singing in their weird language and they on kept chanting my name like possessed rats. All I wanted to do was break up their not so funny song and beat the hell out of them. Sidi read my mind and dragged me away from them.

'Come on, Thando, leave them. Don't mind them. They are just a bunch of useless empty heads.'

'Are they, Sidi? Tell me what did they mean? What do the words of the song mean? Tell me,' I fumed filling my bucket with water.

'Why, ugh! Don't mind them, dear. It's nothing, just silly girlish taunts, you know, hey'.

Sidi was lying to me and I just wanted to baptise the truth out for her in the water hole, but I didn't. It frustrated me every time she had to make up excuses not to tell the truth.

'Cruel pigs they are. Very cruel,' Sidi cursed, filling up her bucket also.

We mounted them on our heads and started the walk back in silence. Each of us was battling with thoughts, yet we could not voice them. I knew that one way or the other, those girls said something that had to do with me being in the Abiyosa plantation and I was itching to know what it was.

As the days went by, my life at the plantation took a turn for the worse. I was treated like a slave. I was made to do all kinds of tasks and there was nothing that I could do about it. Sidi was my pillar and go-to girl. Even though Sadiku, Abiyosa's first wife, tried by all means to keep us apart, her efforts were much like trying to find a tiny needle in the Sahara desert.

"Sidi, I can't do this anymore. My arms are hurting so badly and really I don't think I will be able to lift them tomorrow,' I said throwing down the pestle with all the strength I had left. Sidi did the same as she also threw herself on the ground in a heap.

"Thando, I am also tired, but if that old witch finds us sitting she will fly at us. We actually still have more buckets of millet to pound', she said mournfully.

'I'm done! No one is going to slave drive me against my will. I refuse. Wait 'til she comes and I will tell her where to get off,' I said furiously.

'Oh really? Can you do that young lady?' Shadiku's voice said from behind me.

I sprang up with all my defences on point. Today I was going to give this hag a true piece of my mind. No one was to treat me like a bought commodity.

'Listen here, *magriza*, I am done pounding this millet of yours, done with the crack of dawn wake up call. I am not a rooster. I need my sleep, my rest and this boot camp of yours, rather you take it and shove it up your snot,' I spat like a cornered cobra.

A sounding slap sent a million stars dancing in front of me. Haa! Did this old woman just slap me? I raised my hand to slap back, but it was caught in mid-air.

'You should never hit or talk back at your elders', a deep voice that sent tantalizing sensations through my body said close to my ear. I turned swiftly ready to attack, but what met my gaze made me gasp for breath. My knees turned into jelly, and my tummy did massive somersaults. Boy, the sight before me was fit for a goddess.

CHAPTER ELEVEN

He was tall, dark and heavily muscled. He sported a fresh young beard and his features were curved like the base of a steel pot. The eyes that glared at mine were deep brown, so brown that I thought they were the most marvelous thing I had ever seen. He was shirtless; streaks of sweat rolled down his super-fine body and he had a shirt tied round his trim torso. I can't go down to the greatly toned thighs that were covered by knee-length shorts. The man standing before me was like someone I had seen in the magazines from one of the girls in the mission house.

'Where did you come from? Didn't they teach you how to respect elders? How dare you touch and lay your filthy hands on my Grandmother?' he asked giving my hand a twist.

My dreamy phase about this stranger vanished into thin air and the warrior within me awoke.

'And how dare you lay your filthy, sweaty hands on me? Do you know who I am? Who are you to tell me what and what not to do? And this *magriza* has been pushing me quite a lot. Why *ungabheki indaba zakho*?' (*Why don't you mind your own business?*)

I squared up to him. Sidi was frozen on the spot and her face was clothed in fear.

'Thando, don't. Just keep quiet,' she said, pulling me away.

I pushed her away from me and she landed on her behind.

'Stay out of this, Sidi. No one dares to touch me and twist my arm. He is a man, isnt? I want to show him that I'm Thandolwethu and I'm sick about being treated badly and done with it,' I said, walking close to him and engaging in a full stare contest.

Everything seemed to stop the moment we were level-eyed. Although he was taller than I, I could tell he was still a young bull trying to find his feet in the herd. And well, if he thought I was a lousy heifer, then he had another think coming.

'Move over, bush girl. Village girls like you need to be put in their place,' he said, poking my forehead. He walked towards Sadiku and they walked away towards the huts.

'You Thando, Thando, Thando! This girl will get me killed one of these days, I swear,' Sidi mourned like a widow.

'What? I told you that no one will treat me like dirt anymore and I'm done with this. If they want, they can get their bloody Abiyosa and I will send him off to his ancestors.'

'That man you just insulted is Abiyosa's most treasured possession. He is his late sister's son.'

'So? How is that my concern?'

'Hey, listen up, girly. Your actions have landed us in big, big trouble. Oh! I'm dead today,' she cried.

This girl was such a drama queen. What could Sadiku possibly do? Abiyosa was nowhere to be seen so what could she do to me? The answer to my questions soon came.

I was called to the main hut that evening. As I entered I found it full of village elders, too many to have in one place to be precise. Two women held me down and, oh my! From nowhere I was whipped like a dog that had been caught stealing eggs. At first I was quiet, taking the whips with the strength of a ninja warrior, but as the beating prolonged, I gave in. I screamed like a baby, but no one gave heed to my cries. They kept swearing at me violently and the look on Sadiku's face was of pure bliss. *Nimbaya! Nimbaya!* Witch! one woman kept saying over and over again.

'Sidi was hunched in a corner probably nursing wounds from the lashing she had got. It was my fault that this innocent girl had to pay for my sins. After what seemed like an eternity, they let me go.

'Now listen, young lady from the South. In this place we deal with hooligans like you. This woman is your elder and you will do as told. Hee! What type of bride are you?' one of the village women I recognized asked.

'I'm nobody's bride. Let me go home to my father. You are keeping me here against my will,' I cried.

My tears seemed to amuse them. They laughed their heads off at me.

'Sadiku, I think it's time. The time has arrived for this wretched girl to assume her duties in this homestead properly. You have been putting them off for quite a while, but now is the time. It will be a full moon in the next few days and it's the right time,' one of the women said.

'What...what do you mean, Granny?' I asked, my voice catching in my throat.

'Hehehe. Now she is your Granny? You are getting married to the landlord in the next full moon.'

Married? So soon? Darkness engulfed me and I fell into a dark pit.

I woke up in a dark room. Sidi was kneeling beside me slowly mopping my forehead with a wet cloth. My body hurt a lot from all the lashes I had received, yet the pain was nothing compared to the one I felt in my heart. Ever since I had stepped into this homestead, I had turned this lovely girl's life upside down, yet she still stood by me. I sat up slowly, wincing at the pain that shot through my body.

'Relax, dear. Let me rub all this ointment on you. You will feel better soon enough.'

'But Sidi, you are also hurt. How can you take care of me when we are in the same pain?' I asked, pulling her hand off my arm.

'Hmm. What can I say? Maybe because you are the stupidest idiot I've ever seen and met? But Thando, my buttocks are bruised because of you. When will you learn to close that mouth of yours? Many a time have I warned you, but ehh, this southern girl, I give up,' she chuckled.

That was Sidi for you. She always found a way to make a tense situation seem like a huge joke. That was one of the things I liked about her, apart from her taking the fall for me all the time. I wanted to ask her about the handsome stranger I had met and who I strongly felt was to blame for the lashing that we got, but I stopped myself. That would be news for another day because I needed to plan my revenge properly. If those village women thought they had tamed me, they surely had another think coming. I wasn't called Thandolwethu for nothing. I was my mother's child and my father's daughter. Revenge was my middle name.

The news about the lashing I had been given soon spread all over the village. I was the disciplined bride to be and every woman used each opportunity to actually gossip about it. If it wasn't for Sidi who always calmed me down, I would have gone off the rails. I began to adhere to whatever Sadiku wanted and I did all the tasks set upon me with a calm face yet a vengeful heart.

I had gathered that the handsome stranger was Nwaluku, Abiyosa's nephew, and he had come to visit and stay for the wedding. I don't know what was going on with me, but each time he was close to me I felt really funny. The anger and resentment that I had towards him would vanish the minute he stood in front of me. To make matters worse, he had apologised for getting me lashed and amazingly I forgave him. Having him around the homestead made some of the heavy tasks set upon Sidi and me much easier. He took it upon himself to assist us and I slowly warmed up towards the boy.

'So aunt, are you ready for the pending wedding?' he asked as he chopped the wood for us.

Sidi broke out in hoots of laughter.

'Now that is very rude. I'm not your aunt,' I said irritably. I hated how he addressed me formally and acted as though I was some wasted old woman. Such a good question he had asked, but I just didn't want to dwell much on it. My life was about to take a turn for the worse and there was nothing I could do about it.

CHAPTER TWELVE

He stood legs akimbo, towering over me like Zeus over Athens. His presence sent chills all over my body and I found myself shaking as if I had been dunked in a tank full of ice. This was the man who had taken my life away, taken my joy and most of all made my family turn their backs on me. Abiyosa. The bitter taste his name left on my tongue was worse than having to eat poisonous fungi all my life. Yet here he was, my supposedly wedded husband. He just stood looking down on me as if he were some goblin who had made it to a cave full of gold.

'Beautiful... marvellously beautiful,' he said, grabbing a handful of my afro hair and pulling my neck back. I whined in pain, but returned his stare in this dimly lit room.

'How I've waited for this day to come, to collect my debt in full. Oh my! I was getting tired of waiting, waiting for you to be fully mine, mine, mine, mine,' he said roaring in evil laughter.

Something in me snapped and my palm connected with his cheek. Instead of being stunned by my sudden attack, he merely let go of my hair and laughed hysterically.

'Feisty... That's how I like my women, but I have been unfortunate to get only dummies. Now I have you and you are kindly mine,' he said, pushing me hard.

I hit the wall with the back of my head and the pain was so much I felt my world spin. He came over me, running his hands over my face, down to my breasts. His hand closed over my left breast and he squeezed it tightly just as one would squeeze juice out of an orange. The pain shot to my head, drawing tears to my eyes.

'Stop. Don't do this. You are hurting me,' I cried.

'Oh, now the ice queen feels pain? This is not your father's house. This is my house. I own you and you belong to me now and forever,' he said, hate making his eyes glitter like dew drops.

This was the monster I had been dreading, yet now that I was faced with him, I was just helpless. He shoved me and I lay flat on my back. He came over me and his weight closed in on me. I drummed my fists on his chest, but it was more like trying to break down an ice wall with a toothpick. Grabbing the cloth that housed my breasts, he pulled it off leaving them exposed. An evil smile came over his face as he lowered his foul smelling mouth to them and he bit me. I yelled in pain, but his other hand muffled my scream.

'Shut up, bitch. You know what you came here for. You are my wife and I will do whatever I want with you'.

This man was not joking. He was set on collecting his payment, but I was not going to let him take my womanhood speedily.

'Oh, I'm so sorry. Please don't hurt me. I will do whatever you want, but please don't hurt me,' I said letting my crocodile tears get to him.

I saw him wince and I knew I had struck a nerve.

'Don't cry, princess. As long as you do whatever I want, all will be well. I don't like people who don't do what I want and what makes me happy. Now take off your clothes. I never got the chance to see the merchandise that I purchased through your father's carelessness.'

I obliged and took off the little clothing that I had on me. I was left covered in beads that adorned my neck, wrists and ankles. As if seeing a naked body awoke some devil in him, he ripped his clothes off and was soon naked in front of me. He was heavily set, his manhood stuck out like a huge maize cob ready to be harvested. There was no way I was letting that monster deflower me.

'Come, come to me, Thando. Come pay me my dues, come do your duty,' he said lying back, his manhood sticking out rigid. I raised my knee and aimed it to his manhood. I heard the snap as it connected. That sent the message home. He groaned and rolled into a ball, gasping for air.

'If you think you are going to have me this easy, you are mistaken,' I said, kicking him hard. I raced for the door, undid the bolt ready to flee. This was my chance to make my escape and get away from this beast whilst he was still down. As I stepped out of the hut, I ran straight into the arms of a guard armed with a huge panga. He pushed me back into the hut, closed and bolted the door from the outside.

'You wretched witch. Today I will teach you a lesson. Today I will show you who I really am,' he said as the back of his hand connected with my face. I fell heavily, hitting my forehead on the wall. His leg connected with my stomach sending excruciating bolts of pain. I screamed in agony. Next came the fists. He battered me black and blue, all the time cursing at me. It was as though a demon had taken over his senses. If this is what an erection did to a man, then God had made a mistake by giving men a penis. Abiyosa was a monster, not just a monster, but a horny one too.

'Scream all you want. No one will hear you. You are mine and you will obey me,' he said, spreading my legs apart.

What followed next, even if I describe it to you, you will never understand. He shoved his huge mandingo manhood into my innocent pure vagina, not caring that I was a virgin. I felt the tight walls of my vagina crumble, felt as if my flesh was being torn at by some animal claws. The pain shot straight to my brain, causing me to have a splitting headache, yet he did not stop. He pounded, he shoved and he thrust deeply inside me sending shock waves up my pelvis. Was this what love making was? Was this what all women felt on the day they lost their innocence? All these questions ran through my mind as I lay rigid as a log while Abiyosa deflowered me and took away my pride as a maiden. I recited the Hail Mary over and over again as the nuns had taught me to do in times of hardship, but it seemed as if the holy virgin was on vacation as my endless prayers were not answered. My breasts felt as if they were on fire and ready to fall off as he grabbed and pulled at them. After what seemed like eternity, he rolled off me and lay panting beside me. I neither moved nor rolled away. I lay in a hunched heap, tears rolling down my face, the volcano between my legs burning badly and soaked in blood.

'Your father gave me a good bargain. A virgin to satisfy me every night. You and I will always be together', he said breathing heavily.

Those words did not make an impact on me, I was numb.

If I thought that Abiyosa was done with me, I was mistaken. The torture went on throughout the entire night.

64

He raped me as much as he wanted, each time inflicting a new level of pain. The strength to fight had left me and all I could do was just lie lifelessly and let him do as he wanted. My body was vandalised and brutally tormented. It was the early hours of morning when he left the hut, leaving me foul-smelling of his seed and blood. I lay unmoving for a while until I was sure he had gone, and then I crawled to a corner and cried bitterly.

Why? Why had my father chosen this destiny for me? Why had mother let them do this to me? All the questions swam in my mind, yet I could not find any answer for them.

At the crack of dawn, when the sky was beginning to grey in anticipation of its soulmate to kiss the earth with light, the door opened and someone came through shutting it behind them.

'Please, not again; please, I beg of you. Please spare me,' I cried covering my face.

'It's me, Sidi. I will never hurt you.'

I looked up into Sidi's bloodshot eyes. She had been crying; that was evident. She came close and put her arms around me. I gasped in pain.

'What has this monster done to you? What has he done to you, Thando,' she sobbed pulling the blanket away from me. I was covered in bruises, my cheek was swollen and I felt the fire between my legs. Sidi had brought with her a bucket of warm water. From her skirt, she took out a packet of herbs and added to the water. Patiently she began to wipe me down, taking care not to cause me pain. Why was this girl like this? Why was she always by my side like a sister? She was not family to me, yet in a space of time, she had even replaced my own mother. With the patience of a clucking hen, she cleaned me and dressed me in clean clothes. As she took the clothes I had worn the night before, I stopped her.

'Don't take them away. Don't throw them out, but keep them in a safe place for me. Keep them unwashed, Sidi.'

'Thando, but... '

'Sidi, please do it for me,' I said, tears rolling down my cheeks.

She left the hut with her own flow of fresh tears glimmering on her face.

Night after night Abiyosa brutally raped me and every morning Sidi came to pick up the pieces. Sadiku kept preaching the gospel of how a wife should behave and all her duties. She kept me busy with all house chores and made sure every night she adorned me beautifully to await Abiyosa. Even though he spent most of his time in the homestead, I tried to avoid him as much as I could, but at meal times I was forced to eat with the whole family. Nwaluku remained a friend, but not even a single day did I let it show to him that his uncle was abusing me. Sidi was stuck to me like glue; she had become a sister I never had.

Thinking of sisters, I always wondered how Aunt Nomsa was and how my baby sister Buhle was doing. Thinking of her brought me heartache as I feared she was also destined for the same fate as mine.

Everyone in the Abiyosa homestead expected me to get pregnant sooner or later, but when I got my periods it infuriated Abiyosa such that he gave me the lashing of my life.

'You should be pregnant by now; you should bear me a son,' he roared at me as he sent the whip cracking.

Foolish man! Did he think I was so naive and stupid to fall pregnant for him? I was never bearing a child for him and would never. After the night he had brutally taken my innocence and soiled my clothes with blood, I had sent Sidi with them to the one trusted person I knew would help her, the stranger on the road, the old lady who had housed my brother and me on our way to the Abiyosa plantation. Giving away all my jewelry, I had paid for herbs that would prevent me from falling pregnant and, try as he might, as long as I took the herbs, falling pregnant would be a dream for him. You might wonder how I could pull such a stunt easily, but with Sidi as my main helper it was easy. She always warned me that one day I would be caught out, but I was determined to deprive this monster of the joys of a son as long as I could. I was ready to take any measure to make sure that he never fathered a child with me.

Abiyosa had broken me, but he had not broken the spirit within!

CHAPTER THIRTEEN

My life kept spiraling out of control and there was nothing I could do about it. Abiyosa inflicted pain on me day in, day out, night after night; yet I took it silently. My body had suddenly managed to switch itself to numb mode each time he touched me and shoved his mandingo penis up my vagina. I was determined not to give him what he wanted no matter the pain he made me feel. His dream of an heir was far-fetched and I got a kick out of seeing the efforts he put in raping, knowing that his seed was bouncing against a muti-proof wall. Nwaluku and Sidi were my solace, though many a time I sensed that there was something these two were hiding from me, but I couldn't put my finger on it.

As if watching me like a hawk was not enough, Sadiku gave me the responsibility of being the one to accompany Abiyosa on his many trips to the big town. At first it shook me, but with time I came to know the reason why she sent me. Abiyosa was illiterate and he wanted me to come with him so that I could sign for him and read some of the English words he found difficult. I wondered how he did all his business before, but I guess since everyone feared him, it was easy to get trustworthy people working for him.

It was on one of his many trips to the city that I learned a few interesting things about the family I was married to. Abiyosa had just closed a cattle deal and was sitting by a roadside inn with two of his friends. Alcohol filled the table and after a few bottles too many, they started to chat, ignoring my presence.

'My friend, tell me your secret. How in the name of the gods did you manage to marry a second wife? I mean we all know what a dragon you married,' one of his friends named Olekunlu asked.

Loud laughter erupted from the group of four setting two birds that were picking up crumbs flying off to safety. I could tell that the African brew was starting to get the better of them.

'Olekunlu, my friend, who am I? I am the owner of this entire place, the Lord to the many desperate fathers willing to sell their children,' he said scornfully shooting a hateful look in my direction.

That look I knew too well. It was the look that meant that tonight you better give me an heir or you are dead meat. I dutifully looked away and pretended to be browsing the old newspaper that was used as a table cloth.

'Sadiku had no choice but to agree. Years on end she had been just a cow set on a feeding scheme and yet did not produce Milo's,' he said, taking a long sip from the calabash before them.

'Then why did you marry her? You could have found any girl or woman you wanted, but you ran to that plain field,' one of his friends put in.

'My man, what was I to do? Bulldoze and kick luck when it presented itself before me? There was no way I was not going to marry Sadiku, not with her wealth ready to come by me.'

Sadiku and Abiyosa? Euw, that gave me the jitters. Through their loud banter I gathered that Sadiku was Abiyosa's wife. She was much older than he and in spite of her age, Abiyosa had married her for her wealth. Although this marriage never produced a child, Abiyosa gained

Shadiku's wealth after her father died making him the most powerful man in the area.

I could not believe that he allowed his friends to speak ill about Sadiku. Sadiku, the one woman who kept his house afloat. I burned with fury, but there was nothing I could do about it. I promised myself to get the whole story. After what seemed like ages, we left for the plantation. Due to his intoxication, the drive back home was bumpy and it took longer than anticipated such that we arrived when the sun was long asleep. During the ride, Abiyosa made it clear that I was not going to pass the night peacefully. As soon as we were behind closed doors, he brutally pushed me against the wall. I hit it hard with my forehead, but dared not express my pain as seeing me in pain made him more savage.

'Tonight you will give me an heir, an heir to salvage all this wealth, Thandolwethu,' he growled like a dog with rabies.

With his foul breath inches from my face, he maneuvered his way throughout my body. I could not feel the pain any more as my body had grown used to it. I was just numb and could not feel anything, yet my other hidden sense was overworking. After what seemed like hours he rolled off, leaving me soaked in his seed and sweat. The alcohol kicked in quickly and in a matter of seconds he was snoring like a broken down truck. Quietly I snuck out of his hut and went to the one where I knew a pair of friendly faces would be awaiting me. Sidi's hut was my home and I never spent a night too many in Abiyosa's hut unless forced to.

As I approached the hut I could hear some voices and one voice sent tremors through my entire body. I entered the hut with my head bowed low and readily fell into Sidi's arms.

'Don't cry now, Thando. You cannot do this every night he hurts you,' Sidi whispered.

She was right, it was time I toughened up and endured all that Abiyosa sent my way. I really did not want Nwaluku to see my vulnerable side. Wiping my tears in the semi-dark room, I flashed him a smile and he smiled back. Oh! Good lord, that smile turned my knees to jelly and I could not stop myself from staring at him unblinkingly.

'Hey, blink aunt! You will hurt those big eyes of yours. I'm not a ghost, you know,' he said teasingly.

'Call me your aunt one more time and I will crush you like a roach.'

We all burst out laughing. My ever sweet Sidi had warm water ready for me and I obediently took the basin outside, washed off and scrubbed any smell of the man I loathed off me. Try as I might, I felt he was always all over me like leprosy. After a good cleaning, I rejoined the two in the hut, feeling a little bit refreshed. Nwaluku had brought roasted nuts and dry maize snack from the paddocks and I was more than happy to indulge. Conversation was slim as each one of us was battling with many individual thoughts. The attraction between Nwaluku and me was very strong and I struggled to swallow the dry maize snack. Sidi came to the rescue by ordering him to go to bed as it was getting extra late. When he was gone, she turned towards me with questioning eyes.

'You like him, isnt? Thando, that is very dangerous. Hee! Does this foreign girl want to kill me?'

'Yes, Sidi, I like Nwaluku. I like him a lot, yet I know he sees me as his aunt and that's really stupid.'

'No, that's not stupid. It's meaningful. Do you think Sadiku will spare you if she found out? What about your husband? Do you think he will spare you? Young lady from the south, be careful. Stop poking at a fire that will burn you,' Sidi fumed at me.

Many a time she had quietly advised me. Today it seemed that she really meant what she said. Her voice had an edge of fear and that worried me a lot. Did I just overstep a boundary with her? I wondered, or was she interested in Nwaluku herself and was bent on playing defence on me? I knew that was a stupid thought, yet I just felt as if nothing I wanted was coming my way.

I gathered my mat and after putting out the fire, I cuddled close to Sidi who had suddenly gone to voicemail. I knew that maybe I had gone a little bit over the top, but what could I have done? Could I run to Sadiku and say I'm in love with your nephew?

Sleep came by with great difficulty. I had lain wide awake battling my discovery about Sadiku, my feelings for Nwaluku and my fresh fight with Sidi. How could one's life be so twisted and complicated, I wondered. Finding it hard to sleep without reconciling with my best friend, I nudged her awake.

'What now, Thando? Can't you let me sleep without your drama antics?'

'Sorry, Sidi. Really I am.'

'Apologising doesn't suit you. It makes you seem weak. Now get your ass to dream land and stop kicking me with your long feet,' she mumbled.

I smiled into the darkness, knowing that she was no longer angry.

'And oh, Thando, he likes you too,' she said covering herself with the blanket.

The cockerel had come to roost and this hen was determined to impress.

CHAPTER FOURTEEN

My infatuation with Nwaluku kept me going. A day spent without seeing his face felt incomplete. Sidi tried by all means to keep my wild teenage feelings in check, but in vain. I made sure to do all of Shadiku's chores in hope that even once I would get a smile of approval from Nwaluku's aunty, but hey, it was like barking up a rock. On many occasions I had tried to ask Sidi about Sadiku, but she made it clear to me that the subject was off limits. On the other hand, even though I knew he liked me, Nwaluku acted indifferently with me and it drove me up the wall. As for my husband, it was fun to see his frustration month after month whenever I had my periods. It killed him and once I heard him mumbling that maybe he was shooting blanks and should seek the help of a seer.

It was on a sunny day that I found myself on the grinding stone working my hands off to the bone. Nwaluku and Sidi had been sent to give far off relatives some grain and it meant that they would arrive home later that evening. The yard was as quiet as a grave, with only an occasional cock chasing a hen in seek of coitus. Sadiku had tasked me to grind some millet as she wanted to prepare Abiyosa's favourite meal. A shadow fell over my hunched back and I looked up.

'Hmm. You are surely getting the hand of this grinding stone. In no time you will be doing it as well as Sidi does,' Sadiku said, as she inspected the fine powder between her fingers.

Did my ears hear right or Sadiku had just complimented me? Grabbing the bull by the horns, I decided this was the perfect time to test the waters.

'Aunt Sadiku, if I may,' I said.

'Yes, my child, you can ask away,' she said politely.

I realised the current was still moderate and perfect for me to press on.

'Will you tell me more about this place? It's been a year now since I came as a bride and no one has ever bothered to tell me about the happenings of this place,' I asked in my so-called most respectable voice, not that I had one, but that particular time I had to try.

'This place my child is like heaven and hell at the same time.'

'What do you mean?'

'Oh, you young folk are so naive. You rarely notice things before you. I mean that at times this place can be good to you and bad to you. It can yield fruitfully and can be harsh like a whip,' she said.

I pressed more buttons and soon she was telling me about all the happenings and customs of the place. I felt drawn and attracted to her, not because she was talking to me, but because Nwaluku's aunt was finally talking to me. Maybe I felt that I was a step closer to being accepted by her, not as Abiyosa's wife, but as Nwaluku's rose.

As she chattered away, my mind drifted in wild imagination. There I was adorned to the toes in the most beautiful beads standing beside my African Prince Nwaluku. He was looking so handsome and majestic. His eyes were filled with love and his hand rested on the big bulge that protruded before me. Sadiku was singing and ululating her heart off as she gave us our blessings and I could see old Abiyosa shrivelled and stuck on the chair with wheels that the mission gave to impaired people. I chuckled at the thoughts that painted such a vivid picture.

'What so funny about drought?' Shadiku's voice quickly erased my images.

Damn it! Did she have to interrupt me?

'Nothing, aunt, nothing at all. Tell me, aunt, how did you come to stay at this place? I mean, you are from up East isnt?' I asked hesitantly.

Sadiku's face turned sour as if gallons of lemon juice had been forced down her throat.

'I'm not from the East. Have you been talking to Sidi?' she asked, her tone changing.

'No aunt, but I just wanted to know why you did not tell me that you are Abiyosa's first wife,' I said boldly.

Sadiku's face turned deathly white and she shot me an angry look. I shuffled backwards on my buttocks my heart racing.

'Who told you that? Who told you? Is it Sidi? Oh! I'm going to kill that girl today,' she said picking up her skirts and walking away.

I got up quickly and blocked her way.

'You are not going to leave without answering, you old lady. Why didn't you tell me,' I asked, my confidence going overboard.

If I had known what was to follow, I wouldn't have dared to question her. Sadiku's palm connected with my cheek and I dived into the hot African dirt like a lizard that has been swatted off the wall. She bent down and pulled me up by the ears.

'How dare you? How dare you, Thandolwethu?' she spat at me, shaking me like a water reed.

'How dare I what old woman? I need to know and please,' I shot back.

'*Chepe msichana! Ambao unafikiri ni?*', she shouted at me. (*Mannerless girl, who do you think you are?*)

Now all networks went off for me because I did not understand what she meant by that. Each time she was mad she would switch to her native language.

'I need to know, and if you are cursing, right back at you, old woman.'

'*Ikiwa kuuliza mimi kwamba, nitakuna,*' she said aiming her foot at me. (*If ever you ask me that, I will kill you.*)

I dodged and rolled away. I bumped against Nwaluku's legs. I looked up at him and our eyes met and I could see the fury in his eyes. He walked past me and squared up with his aunt.

'*Mikono off shangazi! Kuondoka Thando peke,*' he said to his aunt in a tone I had never heard him use before. (*Hands off aunt. Leave Thando alone.*)

I stood up and cowered behind him. There was no knowing what Sadiku would throw at me. Rather it hit Nwaluku than me.

'*Msichana hii ni heshima* Nwaluku. I just can't deal with her behaviour,' Sadiku screamed back. (*This girl is disrespectful, Nwaluku.*)

'*Kuacha ni na wala hit yake!* Just stop it'. (*Stop it and do not hit her.*)

Now this was getting interesting to me. Here were two people fighting each other over me and I didn't understand a single word they were saying. All I could figure out was that Nwaluku was defending me.

'*Nini yeye na wewe? Nini yeye na wewe* Nwaluku?,' Sadiku shouted. (*Who is she to you?*)

'*I upendo shangazi yake na nataka yake!*,' Nwaluku said putting his hands around me. I sank deep into his embrace knowing that Sadiku would not get to me. I saw the old woman's face turn pale with fear. (*I love her, aunt, and I want her.*)

'*Huenda miungu ndiri ila mimi*,' Sadiku said in a shivering voice. (*May the good gods save me.*)

'*Ni shangazi was kadli i upendo Thando*,' Nwaluku said quietly, lowering his head. (*It's true aunt, I love Thando.*)

'*Kutoka nje ya macho Nwaluku yangu, kwenda!*.' Sadiku said angrily. Nwaluku let go of me and quietly left. (*Get out of my sight, Nwaluku.*)

'Young woman, follow me, now!'

Now I knew I was way deep in trouble and I didn't know why Nwaluku had decided to confront his aunt. It was good in a way, yet now he had gone off leaving me to face the wrath of this old woman. I now felt what Sidi always felt each time I landed her in hot soup. Now the tables had turned and Nwaluku had left me to fix the mess he had caused.

Sadiku took me to her hut and shut the door behind her. My heart was just about to jump out of my chest. There was no telling what this crazy old woman would do to me and being alone without my side kick made it worse.

'Sit down,' she said pointing to a mat by the corner.

I obeyed like a well-mannered child. Already she was as mad as a jilted cobra and I was not going to add more fuel to the fire that I had caused with my big mouth. Sidi had always warned me about talking too much and I had never listened.

'You want to know my relationship with your husband, do you?'

'Your husband, Granny,' I corrected.

'Can you shut up for a while, Thandolwethu? Hee. *i mikono off wewe!.*' (*I wash my hands of you.*)

'I'm sorry, Granny. I didn't mean to interrupt,' I said quietly.

'Shut up!' she barked at me.

I nodded and waited for her to continue. She cleared her throat before she spoke.

'What I am about to tell you should stay within these walls, Thando. Never are you to relate it to anyone. If you do, then you would have dug both our graves.'

'Yes, Granny.'

'Now listen to me. This is my story,' she said, clearing her voice. 'I was much older than you are now when my father brought Abiyosa home. He was the loving uncle and everyone adored him. I always wondered why father was so eager to work with the stranger that had arrived in our village and curious as I was, I always asked father what he did with this man and why. As years went by, Abiyosa became more of a family member and father began to trust him with matters of the family. I was always sceptical about his interests in our family, but as a girl child, I had to know my place and not question everything that father did.

As the years went by, Abiyosa began not only to be a regular visitor during meal times, but also began to spend nights and sometimes seemed under the disguise that he was helping father with farm matters. After a while, father appointed him as his chief overseer of the farm since he was a wizard with managing people. That infuriated my uncles, yet father always had the last word. Abiyosa not only managed the farm and finances, but began to create a rift between father and his brothers in such a way that in a short space of time a huge feud had erupted which led to the brotherhood breaking up. To cut a long story short, he began to show interest in me, but since I was already promised to somebody else, he had no way of getting me to change my mind, or at least so I thought. The night he chose to kill my husband-to-be was the very night he poisoned father.'

Sadiku paused as she became overcome by emotion. I looked at this woman I had always seen as an iron fist and my heart bled for her.

'What didn't you tell the people what had happened? Surely someone would have listened, isnt?'

'Yes, someone could have listened, but everyone feared Abiyosa. Rumour had it that where he came from, sacrifice of humans was as easy as sacrificing a sheep, so no one dared to oppose him. My uncles readily surrendered to him and when he asked for my hand in marriage, they obliged. Here I was, an almost-bride turned widow turned bride in a week. Fear made me marry him but wit made me deny him a child, just like you have been doing,' she said fixing me with stone cold eyes.

'Child... me... denying... ah, what are you saying?' I stammered.

Sidi was going to be dead. How dare she tell Sadiku about the herbs?

'I know it all, Thando; the herbs you have been drinking.'

'Umm. It's nothing, aunt. Nothing like that. I only drink medicine to help me with indigestion.'

'*Msichana,* I wasn't born yesterday; I know all.'

'Please do not tell him. He will kill me,' I begged her.

She gave a half-laugh, half-snort before she answered.

'You are already dead, my dear. You are coo-coo with Nwakulu and that is a one way ticket to hell.'

'Aunt, I... ,' I stammered.

'Don't explain. The idiot loves you and if both of you have death wishes, go ahead, but leave Sadiku out of it,' she said teasingly.

Who could have thought *magriza* and I would be sitting together this way. Her story made me realize I had misjudged her, yet she wasn't on a free mode yet. I was not going to just blindly trust her. No way.

'So do not relate whatever I told you to anybody else. Do not even dare show that you know anything. The time has come to take back what is mine, to avenge my lost love. I need you in one piece to do so, do you hear me?' she asked sternly.

I nodded in agreement.

'Now up on your buttocks and pound more meal. I need fresh ground meal for tonight's meal. And no chatting up,' she said, shutting the door behind her.

I sat stunned and overcome with emotions. Did Sadiku just make a pact with me? Did she just make peace with me and maybe give tiny blessings about Nwaluku? I wondered. I picked up my mortar and pestle and proceeded to the pounding courtyard, my heart singing blissfully. Nwaluku had stuck his neck out for me, I knew Sadiku better and I was so ready to play this game with Abiyosa. If he thought he had me, then he had another think coming.

As I pounded the meal, my heart sang a song that only I could understand. I felt a load had been taken off my shoulders, yet something was amiss. I didn't want to put my trust in Sadiku no matter how sad her story was. What if it was just a big, fat tale? What if it was a way to test my loyalty to Abiyosa and Nwaluku was in on it?

'If you are not careful you will grind your fingers,' a voice that sent electrical shots throughout my body said.

Nwaluku. He was a silhouette of magnificence, a wild stallion that needed to be tamed, and a wild boar that belonged to no herd. Looking at him made me feel weird and his scent always sent me swooning and weak-kneed.

'If I pound them, then you will have to do all my house chores,' I said flashing him a smile.

'You wish,' he said, patting my head as he moved away towards the kraals.

His touch, tiny touch sent my blood beyond boiling point. Control, Thando, control, I chided myself.

My life was beginning to take a new turn and I was more than ready for the battle. The lines had been drawn and the war had begun.

CHAPTER FIFTEEN

The game had changed now. Instead of being the hunted, I was now the hunter and my prey was not an easy one to stalk. Abiyosa seemed to sense the change in me and when he mentioned it to Sadiku, she advised him to lay low on me for a bit. She told him that I was succumbing to the pressure that he put on me towards having a baby and that if a woman is pressurised that much, conceiving would be a hard task. That kept him at bay for a few weeks, apparently to let me relax and heal from his brutal love making. Nwaluku and I met secretly, always under Sidi's watchful eye. He made me laugh and he made me feel wholesome. Each and every time he was with me, I felt as if heavens had opened up and I was a welcomed guest. Although we had the old lady's permission, we were not allowed to be seen together as much as we wanted or people would start talking.

It was on a very stormy afternoon while I was sitting in my room that I opened the little envelope that my dear beloved friend had given me. I took out the wad of notes and stared at them blankly. If I had been at the mission, this would have been a huge jackpot for me. Thinking of the mission brought tears to my eyes. I had missed a year in school and was already missing another. Tears of frustration rolled down my cheeks at the misfortune that had befallen me. Only two people were to blame, just two people, Abiyosa and Paulina.

You might wonder why I'm blaming Paulina instead of my father, but I believe she instigated father on the loans and her eagerness to get rid of me as quickly as possible was all I needed as proof. I was going to get my revenge on her, but at the moment I had to focus on the task at hand.

Sadiku wanted me to hold off having a baby for as long as I could, but we both knew that it was a hard task. Soon it was going to be another full moon and already the village people were talking. Once a group of old cronies had waylaid me on my way to the river.

'Greetings, young bride,' one had said.

'Hello, Grandmother.'

'My child, when are you going to give us something to play with?'

'Something to play with? Are you not too old to play with toys, Granny,' I said scornfully, knowing exactly what she meant by that.

'Hehehe. This uncultured girl. Is this how you talk to your elders? Hawu! Sadiku has lost her touch.'

'Listen here, *magriza*. My advice to you is that you should focus on your home issues rather than on mine. Be careful. I might end up being your sister wife, since old men seem to like me,' I said, sashaying my now blossomed behind, not giving a care in the world.

I had become bold; so daring that I felt untouchable. Back chatting had become my thing and every woman in the village had come to know that I, Thando, did not take any shit from anyone.

A knock brought me from my own world and Sidi came in through the doorway. She bore a basket laden with all sorts of wild fruit. This girl really knew the way to my heart. Fruit and I were mutual lovers, especially the native fruit that was common in my home village, the *umkhomo* from the queen of trees, the baobab tree.

'And you wonder why I love you so much?' I asked practically grabbing the basket from her.

'Hey, hold your horses. At least say thank you, Sidi; you are the bomb, Sidi,' she said pushing me slightly.

It was as if she was talking to a deaf and dumb person. Like a monkey that had been starved for many days on end, I was stuffing my face with the sour *umkhomo* fruit, not showing any shyness at my greediness. Poor girl. I bet she had never seen a woman who had an appetite for such a sour fruit the way I did.

'Are you sure it's just a normal liking for this sour fruit of yours or you are already a duck sitting on eggs?' she asked as she cut through my feast like a sword.

I choked on the fruit and wild coughing followed. I grabbed the jug of water and emptied it down my throat.

'*Wena mntwana! Ufuna ukungibulala angithi?*' (*You Baby! You want to kill me, huh?*) I gasped for breath.

'Now you have started cursing me with that tongue-clicking language of yours. Are you sure you are not pregnant?' she asked a sly smile dancing on her lips.

'Pregnant? Me? With whom? How many times have I told you that if it's not Nwaluku then it's nobody? I will not bear my fruit for an old fox,' I said irritably.

'Hmm alright. I was just asking. Of late you are glowing a lot,' she said jokingly.

Oh my! Sidi always knew how to rub and push my buttons the wrong way, yet she was one person who never sugar-coated anything from me. I pushed the basket towards her and we silently devoured the fruit like a pack of hungry hyenas on its prey.

We exchanged chatter as we indulged, but one thing kept me drifting away from our chatter. Abiyosa was going to another district that evening and he was kind enough to let me stay behind. That made me happy, although when he had told me, I had put on my not-so-happy face and sulked like a witch that had failed to make a grade in witch school. He had tried to explain about his work even though I knew he was off to see some mistress of his. My sulking was just my cover up, for the minute he was gone I was going to be as free as a butterfly and fall into the arms of my Nwaluku. After some convincing I had agreed to his journey and yes, after being promised a fat goat being added to my already growing kraal of smelly goats as a present.

Nightfall seemed to be ages away, but as soon as the sun was slowly caressing the beautiful landscapes, Abiyosa came into my hut and bade me farewell. As a dutiful wife, I kept my eyes downcast and bade him farewell too.

'Be good. When I come back we will continue to try and make an heir. You have to give me an heir,' he practically growled in my ear. I nodded quickly just happy to have him gone. When I saw the back of his truck being swallowed by the cloud of dust, I let out a huge sigh. The lion was off the radar and it was time for the cats to play.

I took out my favorite dress and laid it on the grass mat. Tonight I was going to be with the person who had my heart beating abnormally, my Nwaluku. I had not seen him for many days on end and this was our only chance to be together when the old fox was out of the way. We had already made arrangements. Only Sidi was my confidant; Sadiku had no idea I was about to go against her wishes and do the unspeakable.

I took a long bath and adorned myself with sweet smelling perfume that Abiyosa had given me. I knew he had taken it from his city woman because no one gives a half-empty bottle of perfume as a gift. Nevertheless, I had accepted it and it was going to come in handy tonight. As darkness fell, Sidi came into my room and sat looking at me with dreamy, yet worried, eyes.

'What is it? Loosen up a bit. He is not here and I told Sadiku I will sleep early as I am having a bad headache,' I said, covering my arms with many colored bangles.

'What if she comes to check up on you, Thando?'

'That's where you come in, my friend. You will sleep here tonight and pretend to be me until I come back.'

'Ah ha ha! This girl! If she gets to know, she will kill us, Thando,' she said in her drama queen voice.

'I won't tell if you don't. Didn't you say you will do anything for me?'

I gave her my very sweet and innocent face and she just couldn't resist the charm.

'Okay, but be back before midnight or else,' she said, pushing me towards the door.

'I can't promise, but I will try,' I said while shutting the door behind me.

Outside it was pitch black and for someone afraid of the dark, I was surprised to learn what love did to fear. I stealthily walked around the huts and ducked under the fence onto the pathway that led towards the river. Nwaluku had said he would waylay me on the path, but fear was at the back of my mind. After walking for almost half an hour, I heard a low catcall. I responded with a more feminine one and waited for a response. It came within seconds from some bushes that were grouped into a thicket. As I walked towards them, Nwaluku emerged. As if some force were pushing me, I ran and collapsed into his warm embrace. My body turned suddenly warm as I held him tightly.

'*Ndlovukazi yami,*' ('*My Queen*') he said in an imperfect Ndebele accent, yet music to my ears.

'My Lwuku,' I said, allowing his mouth to hungrily cover mine. I was complete.

CHAPTER SIXTEEN

Chills ran down my spine, sending massive electric sparks throughout my body. My head spun as if I were on a roundabout and couldn't stop it. Nwaluku broke away from me and help me at arms-length. His breathe came in heavy gasps and his eyes burned red with desire. I looked back at him trying to compose the urge to pull him close and feel his body against mine.

'Thando.'

I halted his words with my finger and nodded silently. He was so unsure, but I was sure of what I wanted and I wanted him. Slowly he drew me close, tracing his finger along my cheek until it rested on the tip of my chin. He slowly tilted my head up and brought his lips down on mine. This time he was gentler and composed. Soft as a feather, he planted fairy-light kisses all over my neck, ears and lips. The sensations created by those soft touches made me want to scream out loud and beg him to satisfy the fire that burned in me. I held on to him tightly, breathing heavily like a steam engine. Piece by piece my clothes began to fall away. I clumsily tugged at his shirt, but he stopped me and gave me a look that simply said 'Don't rush. Let me handle this'.

I lay back as he slowly got rid of every cloth that covered me. I was left stark naked except for beads that adorned my wrists and waist. His hand moved over my body like a sculptor admiring one of his fine pieces of art. I wriggled like a worm under his touch, but this man was in no rush to get to the end of the tunnel, to see the light, to satisfy his hunger.

My hands moved as if in clock fashion and I slowly helped him off with his clothes too. If this trip was going anyway, we would rather be on the same boat. As the last piece of clothing fell off Nwaluku, I gave a gasp. Oh! My goodness, he was perfectly made. His chest and torso oozed of male charisma, his thighs were firm and strong and what lay between them, just sucked every single breathe from me. He was beautifully crafted, a stallion that flexes its huge muscles at ease. He possessed a presence that mesmerised me and sent my head spinning.

Nwaluku stood before me clad in his birthday suit. I was stunned at how manly and mature this boy could become in seconds. He held his hands out to me and, as if by a magnetic force, I felt drawn into his embrace. As our bodies came into contact, he groaned softly.

'Are you sure you want this, Thando?' he whispered, uncertainty in his voice.

Oh damn! This guy! Without any answer I pulled him closer and looked into his eyes in the glowing light. I nodded slightly and allowed him to lie me down on the many soft mats he had majestically placed on the floor. As if some sort of demon came over him, he closed his lips on mine with renewed hunger that took my breath away. His lips seemed to have the gift of exploration as they moved from each part of my body like a fine brush. Desire took over me and I drew him down, guiding him to where I wanted him to be, but he wasn't in a rush to grant my wish. I moaned and groaned, begged him to ease the fire that burned between my legs, yet he turned a deaf ear. His hand craftily traced patterns on the inside of my thighs and I let out a muffled scream.

'Please, not any more, Nwaluku, 'I pleaded with him unable to withstand the burn of desire.

'Your wish is my command,' he whispered as he slowly parted my now limp thighs. As he slid in his rock-hard manhood, I completely lost my mind. I died for a moment and I guess definitely went to ancestral lands. The feeling was unlike that which I had been subjected to by Abiyosa. This was what making love felt like. This was what a connection between two people felt like. As our bodies joined in union, I felt my very soul and body merge with Nwaluku's. He looked me deep in my eyes and all I could see was my reflection. Our union was love-filled and desire-borne. No one could take that from us. Nwaluku took my body and made it whole. As he drove deeper and deeper within the cove of my volcano, I willingly arched my hips to meet his demanding hunger. I was his and he was mine.

Our love-making lasted for as long as we could hold on and when he emptied his seed within me, it felt as though our souls were tied with cords of unbreakable vines. I moaned and cried out to him as he scattered his spent energy way deep within me, his moans echoing in my ears. Ours was a union no one would ever break or come between. I held on to him as he lay spent and drained in my arms, sobbing softly with desire.

'I love you, Thando,' he panted heavily.

'And I love you too, Lwuku,' I said, cradling him like a small child in my arms. He lay breathing heavily, his manhood pulsing and vibrating with contentment in my womanhood. Time stood still for us as we lay in each other's arms. Sleep came over us and we drifted into blissful sleep, covered in each other's love.

Throughout the night, Nwaluku and I made love to each other endlessly. It was like a never ending rollercoaster. He took me to heights I had never thought any man would, considering my first time with Abiyosa. My body merged with his easily and we totally spent each other for hours on end. As dawn approached Nwaluku nudged me awake.

'Thando, we have to go back. It's almost dawn,' he said, planting a wet kiss on my lips.

'Is it necessary for us to leave? Can't we stay here for a while or just run away together, Lwuku?' I pleaded, despair sinking into my heart at the thought of having this magical moment cut short.

'I wish we could, but we can't. What we just did can get us killed, my mountain lioness. We need to be cautious and not get caught out. In due time I will take you away from this place and from that monster Abiyosa,' he said, his face clouding at the mention of Abiyosa. I nodded slowly and fell into his arms.

We dressed hastily and went out into the semi-dark of early morning. Birds were chirping lovingly and a few underground creatures scattered from our path ready to start their morning routine of food scavenging. We made it to the river as the horizon turned crimson. I went to some bushes and retrieved a bucket and a dress that I had hidden there the day before. Nwaluku gave me a confused look.

'The bucket?' he asked. Oh my! Did this guy not know that a bucket with water early morning is a good cover? My aunties always did that whenever they sneaked off during the night. Either they would have a bucket or they would come home balancing firewood on their heads. My mothers would never suspect a thing.

'Oh, Lwuku, you will never understand,' I said changing into the dress I had worn the day before. We hurried along the path that led to the watering hole.

'It's best that you go your own way. I can hear voices by the watering hole. I will see you at home,' I said, pushing him towards the path that branched to the Abiyosa plantation.

'But,... '

'No *sthandwa sami (My love)*. We don't want to raise suspicion,' I said, scampering down the slippery path to the watering hole.

A number of village belles were already there, sharing the daily gossip and laughing their heads off. As I approached, their laughter subsided and they gave me knowing stares. I felt that they could see through me and what I had been up to the whole night. Thinking of that, a smile danced on my lips as I reminisced about my wonderful night.

'Why the stares? Have you never seen a married woman by the watering hole in early morning?'

I broke the ice with my bitchy attitude. Ever since I had shown boldness and my ability to kick ass, they knew better than to mess with me.

'Oh no, Thando. We were just wondering why a woman who has everything at her feet could be seen here at this hour. Don't you have maids to fetch water for you? I mean that plumpy Sidi' said one girl who I had seen a couple of times bothering Sidi and actually eyeing my Lwuku.

I walked close to her and leveled my gaze on her.

'*Usufuna ukuphapha angithi?* (*You want to be vigilant, don't you?*) This wondering of yours. Keep it to yourselves unless you want to meet up with *umvundla lo nteletsha bami (my left and right fists)*,' I said, showing them my fists. That broke up the party and they hurriedly balanced their buckets on their heads and hurried off. A chuckle sounded from behind me. I turned and found Sidi unable to stop herself from laughing.

'Ha! You are such a bully? Was there need to scare the poor girls away like that?' she asked, taking my bucket and starting to fill it up.

I sat on the cold sand and stared into space.

'She called you plumpy and no one makes fun of my Sidi.'

'Oh, should I say thank you? Considering that you call me your little piggy whenever I refuse to give in to your crazy demands,' she said.

'That's different. Only I can tease you,' I said, throwing a handful of sand at her. We burst out laughing. Such was the beauty of friendship between us.

We balanced our buckets on our heads and took the path back home. Abiyosa was due that evening and I was not looking forward to it at all. Sidi kept up some chatter as we made our way through the dew-covered path. As much as she wanted to ask about the night I had had, she knew we would need a more secure and secluded place to discuss it.

We got to the compound in record time. Some servants were already busy like worker bees and Sadiku was waiting in front of the main kitchen with her gaze on us. I felt a wave of uneasiness come over me as her eyes drilled unending holes in me. Can she see through me, I wondered.

'Morning, my children. Why the early rise like this? I went to your room and you were nowhere to be seen,' she said taking the bucket off my head.

'Morning, *makhulu*. No, we decided to get the fresh water before the cows could muddy it up,' I said picking up a broom.

'Oh, that's so thoughtful of you my child. So thoughtful,' she said going about her way.

I let out a sigh of relief and looked at Sidi.

She shook her head as if to say 'You are bad at covering up'.

We got on with our chores for the day with my heart singing melodies only I could understand. This new-found love, this definition of true womanhood, had me in cloud nine. My life was complete whenever Nwaluku was with me and even Sadiku noticed the change in me, but I brushed her off with 'Maybe it is that time of month.'

Abiyosa's return minimised my meetings with Nwaluku and even though it killed him to know that I lay underneath an old man every night, he showed great patience.

Abiyosa wanted a child as soon as possible, but I was not going to allow him that, not under the stars. Many times he questioned me about why I was not conceiving as his seed was known for being powerful and each time I had to save my skin by a hook. In the end I resorted to an even more dangerous method. I stopped taking the herbs and asked Sidi to get me something that would definitely get me in trouble if discovered.

'What! Are you out of your mind? The herbs work much better,' she said, her eyes almost falling out of her sockets.

'Sidi, I need this, please. If not for me, do it for Nwaluku. Imagine how it would be if I fell pregnant? Both our lives will be over.'

'No! This time I refuse. Don't involve me, Thando. I don't want to die before I get married.'

'You will die before that because I will kill you myself if you don't help me! Aint you supposed to be my friend and before that A SERVANT OF MINE?' I said, fixing her my authoritative look.

That did the trick. Her face fell ashen like that of a ghost caught trying to climb out of a grave. I hated doing this to her, but I had no choice. Sidi reluctantly took the journey to the small town that was miles away from the Abiyosa plantation. I knew a woman there who was strongly against child marriage and I knew she was one person I could trust to give me what I wanted. It was a risk, but one worth taking. I was not going to fall pregnant for Abiyosa. Not in a million years.

Days went by and new moons followed. Nwaluku and I kept our hideaway a secret and we met occasionally to indulge in the joys of love making. Each time we seemed to be laden with renewed passion and energy. He was a great lover and he completed me. On the other hand, Abiyosa almost cut off his manhood each time a moon passed and I did not fall pregnant. On such occasions, the battering began and he would curse and turn me black and blue over it. I painfully took it all, knowing that I had my own sunshine to look at. One time Nwaluku wanted to confront him after he had given me a blue eye, but I stopped him in time. We did not want to create suspicion around us especially at this crucial time.

On one hot, sunny day, Abiyosa came home earlier than usual bearing a bucket of wild, thorny cucumber. As a dutiful wife, I took them from him and began to slice a few for him. He loved snacking at them especially if salt were added to them. As I sliced open the first cucumber, a wave of uneasiness came over me and I felt dizzy. The ground shifted underneath my feet and a cloud of darkness engulfed me.

I woke up with sharp pain on my head. I blinked painfully into the glare of the light.

'What happened? Ouch! My head hurts a lot,' I said trying to sit up.

'Just keep still. Do not move now,' Sadiku said forcing me back on the grass mat. I looked at her with a confused look. Sidi avoided my gaze and I readily knew something was wrong.

'Can somebody tell me what's going on here? Why are you acting so strangely? Granny, what's happening?' I asked Sadiku, my voice trembling.

She gave me a warm, motherly smile and patted my head affectionately. That was weird even coming from Sadiku and it made me uneasy.

'Thando, my child... '

'Yes, Grandmother,' I answered with my voice dry like that of a desert frog.

'Congratulations, dear, you are with child. You are finally pregnant, Thando,' she said, a huge smile playing on her lips.

My world came crashing down on me as a wave of unconsciousness enveloped me. No way!

CHAPTER SEVENTEEN

I came to with my head throbbing with massive pain as if an elephant had sat on it. As my eyes blinked and I got accustomed to the glare of the sun, I looked nervously around me. Sadiku was kneeling beside me, a contented smile dancing on her lips. She was mopping my forehead with a piece of cloth, humming joyfully. I tried to sit up but she held me down.

'Slowly now, my dear. We don't want to put a strain on the baby, do we?' she asked, helping me.

'Baby? What baby are you talking about? Whose baby?' I asked, panic creeping into my voice.

I looked at Sidi and she nodded excitedly.

'You are with child, dear, and your husband is already on his way. You have finally given him what he has craved for years. You are going to bear him an heir, an heir to this whole estate,' Sadiku said, joy evident in her voice.

How could this be possible? How could I be pregnant for that monster? No! I wanted this thing that was growing within me to be out. I wanted this little devil that was now attached to me to just die, die and be no more. Yes! Yes, it was supposed to die. I had to get rid of this thing in me before it brought me much pain and havoc. As if Sadiku was reading my mind, she cleared her throat before speaking.

'Now that you are with child I will personally monitor you, what you eat and the chores you do. I will leave the night shift to Sidi. I know you girls don't like sharing a room with an old woman. We should make sure you make it to full term', she said, leaving the hut.

I was left with Sidi who gave me a stare that spoke volumes.

'Why, Thando? I asked you not to hurt Nwaluku, but this is what you do? You fell pregnant for that monster. After all Nwaluku has put at risk,' she snarled at me.

'Sidi, let me explain. Please don't misunderstand me. You've got this all wrong,' I said, grabbing her arm.

'Don't touch me, Thando! Just don't. All along I thought you loved him; I thought you wanted him, but no, he was just a toy to you. Congratulations queen bee. Now you can stay with your old man and enjoy your miserable life,' she said, shutting the door with a bang.

I sat dumbfounded and hurt. My own trusted friends and allies had turned their backs on me. I had nowhere to turn.

They say good news hops on one leg and bad news spreads like wildfire. For me this was bad news, but for the Abiyosa homestead it was great news. Soon the whole village knew that Abiyosa was to get an heir. His young bride had finally made him a man amongst men. Nwaluku was one of those who got to know the news first and from his reaction I knew that he did not want to even look at my face. He avoided me at all costs and treated me as a stranger.

On the other hand, Abiyosa was over the moon. He pampered me so much and had a new and much bigger hut built for me. He furnished it for the arrival of the baby. I was now monitored day in, day out. My confidant was mad at me and giving me the cold shoulder and I was lost and stuck with no idea on what to do.

One late afternoon I approached Sidi's hut and knocked softly. No response, so I just let myself in.

'Did I say come in? This is my private dwelling, Mrs. Abiyosa, so until I say come in, you don't,' she snarled at me like a wounded fox.

'Sidi, please hear me out. Please! If I'm forsaken by you, then who will be with me?'

'You should have thought about that before you spread your legs and let that pig plant his seed in you. You should have thought of Nwaluku. He loves you, dammit!'

'I love him too and I know that I am carrying his child!' I said sobbing. Sidi dropped the basin she had in her hands. She came over me with vampire speed.

'Thando, repeat what you just said. No way! Get out of here. Are you sure it's Nwaluku's child?'

I nodded, tears streaming down my cheeks. She gave me a tight hug and planted a sisterly kiss on my forehead.

'I'm sorry I scolded you. I'm sorry. I had no idea.'

She slowly wiped tears from my eyes.

'You didn't listen, dummy. I tried to tell you, but you hated me.'

'Not anymore, my friend. I'm actually going to be an awesome aunt. Yippee!'

'Shh! Walls have ears remember. I need to meet Nwaluku tonight. I need to make him understand. He needs to know.'

'That is easy to sort out. Today Abiyosa is off to the city so you have the whole night to explain to him. But wait, how do you know it's Nwaluku's baby? You have been sampling two bulls at once.'

I knew she was bound to ask me that and my answer was ready. As I had seen how the herbs had got to be a risky method to avoid pregnancy, I had sent Sidi to pick up a package I had ordered from the nearby town. Unknowingly, she had brought me a whole box of female condoms. I resorted to taking them after I stopped taking the pill and the herbs, using a condom whenever Abiyosa was around. The old fool never felt any difference as his main focus was to get me pregnant. Hence, there was no way this child was his. This was Nwaluku's child and I wanted him to know that.

Sidi sat and gave me a ghost ashen look.

'Haa, Thandolwethu! You are something else. I really give up.'

'What choice did I have? It was either him or Nwaluku and I wanted it to be Nwaluku and nobody else,' I said, giving her a hug.

She shrugged her shoulders and left the room after assuring me that she would make it possible for me to meet Nwaluku that night.

I had one obstacle in my way. How would I get rid of the two gorillas that slept outside my hut every night since I got pregnant? I had to get rid of them and fast.

With the support of Sidi back in tune, I set about my plan to ditch Abiyosa's guards that slept outside my door. As if he sensed something, Abiyosa had set two guards on me. They followed me everywhere like lost puppies and made sure they hovered around every place where I went. I had tried to question that, but Abiyosa had dismissed me with the fact that he would not let the mother of his heir come to harm.

That noon, when they had taken their lunch break, I saw it as a chance to go and gather what I needed. I ventured into the dense bush that was behind the cattle kraals and came back with a basket of wild mushrooms. These were not edible wild mushrooms, but ones that either put you into a deep sleep or made you hallucinate like a lunatic. At one point I wanted to make these two hallucinate and see their ancestors, but that would bring me unwanted attention. With much care and ease, I prepared one of my best stews and cooked a very delicious meal that was meant for only them.

As night fell, I gingerly carried the two steaming bowls laden with rich food to them. As I had suspected, they gobbled the food like a pair of hyenas on a helpless impala and even asked for seconds. I gladly provided more, cleaning the pot of every scrap of food. I bade them good night as I retired to my hut. They stationed themselves either on each side of the door like gargoyles and started their night shift. Hours went by and still I could hear their distinct chatter. When I heard heavy snores, it was time to go.

I made my way through the darkness towards our hideout. My heart was pounding against my chest like wild African drums. My feet felt heavy as they thundered on the underbrush. I made it to the hut in record time. Nwaluku was already there, his face a state of massive anger. I ran to him and threw my arms around him. He wriggled out of my embrace.

'Don't touch me, Thandolwethu! Just tell me what you want and be gone from here. I'm sure your husband is eagerly waiting for you,' he said, with a voice full of hate.

His words cut through me like a sword.

'Lwuku, please. Why are you being rude to me? Why won't you listen to me? Why won't you listen to what I have to say', I sobbed bitterly.

This was the man I loved, the man I was risking all for, yet he did not want me.

'What's there to explain? You are pregnant with his child. You have given him what I hoped would be mine. You have made him a father. What more is there to explain, Thando,' he shouted, shaking me roughly.

'The child is yours! You are the father, Nwaluku. Only you and nobody else!' I replied.

Time seemed to stand still as Nwaluku's face changed from anger to shock. He scanned my eyes and I returned his gaze, nodding slowly.

'But how? But Thando, Abiyosa and you?'

'The child is yours, Nwaluku. I'm carrying the fruit of our love,' I said.

He came close and held me tightly.

'How is this possible?' he asked.

I briefly explained what I had done and he listened to me with an expression that spelt pure disbelief.

'So that is why I know you are the father,' I said, giving him a hug.

His arms automatically came around me and he hugged me back.

'I'm going to be a father! I'm going to be a father! Thank you, my love. Thank you, Thando.'

He planted kisses all over my face. We fell into each other's arms and got lost in our world. Our love making became a new thing, for on this night, not only did he make passionate love to me, but he made me completely his. Our souls became one, our bodies merged as one. I was content being with the father of my unborn baby.

As we became lost in our own world, a shadow slowly crept away from our hideout and was lost in the darkness.

CHAPTER EIGHTEEN

As dawn broke over the horizon, covering the sky with gay colors, we made our way through the brush covered with sparkly dew drops. We walked in silence, each battling with unknowns within our minds. I wondered how life was going to be with this turn of events. I had a loving man who would go to the end of the world for me. At the same time I had a monster husband who would do anything to keep me right where he wanted me. Life was not going to be a joyride for me but more like a bumpy rollercoaster.

The baby had not only complicated my life but had also surely given me the zest to get out of this place. Although the plantation had become my home, from deep within me I felt that it was a sordid prison.

As we neared the cattle kraals, we parted ways and I sneaked into the yard. Like a ninja, I made my way to Sidi's hut. As I had guessed, she was pacing back and forth like a caged animal.

'It's about time you got here, Thando!' she said, facing me like a fencing master.

'Come on, Sidi, relax. I'm here, aint I?' I answered gingerly.

'If I were you, I would wipe that smug look off your face because your husband is back. I had to rapidly create a story last night that you had taken some medicine before you slept so his disturbing you would not be a good idea.'

'What! Abiyosa is back?' I stammered my eyes popping out.

'Uhm, yes he is, so you better check your behaviour before it's too late. Keep away from Nwaluku and act normal, Thando, or else you will land us all in hot soup,' she said, gathering the mat and blankets she had supposedly put out for me.

Abiyosa doted on me like a mother duck. The food I ate and the chores I did were under the watchful eye of Sadiku and a few village ladies who had been hired to be my women in waiting. Life turned dull and I did not have any time to spend with Nwaluku. One afternoon as I was shelling nuts under the shade of a huge Acacia tree, one of the herdboys in the homestead came running towards me. Without a word, he dropped a tiny, folded paper on my lap. Before I could stop and ask him where it was from, he was long gone. I curiously unfolded the small paper and the word that met my eyes left me speechless. On the small piece of paper were two words roughly scribbled with black charcoal. The small yet alarmingly scary note read 'I know.'

I felt my heart jump right out of my chest. My blood went cold with fear and I nervously looked around to try and locate anyone who was suspicious. Everything seemed normal and nobody seemed to pay attention to anybody.

Who could this person be? What is it that they knew? Why were they playing a hide and seek game? Questions buzzed through my mind like a swarm of flies over excrement.

'You look so flushed, my child. Is everything okay?' one of the ladies who was now responsible for my well-being asked, running her palm over my forehead. I nodded slightly but she didn't buy it and she yelled for Sadiku. Poor old Sadiku came running, almost falling over.

'Now what is it? Can't I enjoy an afternoon nap without being disturbed?'

'Thando is not well, Grandmother. Look at her face. She is sweating up a storm,' the woman said, tilting my chin up and bringing my eyes level with those of Sadiku. Sadiku shook her head in dismay and readily barked out commands to those close by. With much care, I was helped to my hut and made to sit on the mat. More women came in with wet cloth that they placed on my forehead and under my armpits.

'What's eating you up, my child? Don't you know you should not stress yourself in this state? It is not good for you or for the child,' Sadiku said ushering everyone out.

When we were alone she turned to me with an expression that spelt trouble.

'Now out with it, little girl! What got you hyped up this way? Are you trying to kill yourself and my grandson?'

I shook my head in shame wondering if I should tell her about the note I had been given. If I told her she would panic and blow it out of proportion and if I hid it from her she would eventually have my ass for breakfast. Although I trusted Sadiku, I couldn't risk revealing the escapades that I had had with Nwaluku that were unknown to her. I wouldn't risk it until I found out who was behind the note. With a weak smile I assured Sadiku that I would take some rest and not stress.

Left alone I pondered on a plan to get to the bottom of all this. Before doing anything, I had to recruit Sidi. She was the only one who could help me.

As days went by I got more and more notes, always from the same herdboy. Each time I tried to talk to him, he would just hurry off and not tell me what I wanted to know. The notes were always one or two words. After I had received the eighth note, I called Sidi to my hut one afternoon and showed them to her. She sat like an old traditional healer trying to detect a message from the bones. After a while she shook her head in disbelief.

'Hee! Someone is really playing a dirty game with you, Thando. It's going to be dangerous if we don't put a stop to it. I know just how we can catch this person,' Sidi said, grinning.

I knew that evil grin and feared that it spelt utter disaster. With a few days pending before the full moon, we set our plan in motion. If the note writer was not going to come straight to me I was ready to go to him. My lioness mode was on point and I was ready to put a stop to this.

On the night of the full moon, Sidi and I crept silently towards the river where our mystery note writer had said we should meet. Taking advantage of the eerie glow of the moon, we cowered behind trees and avoided the path as much as we could. The fact that I was bulging a bit in front didn't bother me. All I cared for was to silence this mysterious secret admirer who was scaring the pants off me. I had asked Nwaluku to join us, but he had not come so we left without him.

Armed with a knobkerrie just in case we had to beat the truth out of this mystery person, we got to the river in record time. A hooded figure was standing on the river bank with his back towards us. At our approach, he slowly moved off, beckoning with his hand that we should follow him. My instincts gave me a warning, but I shut them down with my mock bravery.

'Thando, I think we should go back. Nwaluku is not here and we can't just follow this person in the dead of night,' Sidi said, her voice laden with nervousness and fear.

'Now don't go soft on me, Sidi, and back out now. We are in this together. You surely won't leave a pregnant woman alone to face whatever monster lurks in the dark, right?'

Sidi shrugged her shoulders and reluctantly followed. We walked for some minutes before we turned a bend. Here the river widened into an open space of sand and there were a few deep ponds scattered about that the herdboys used as swimming pools. It was rumoured that some of them were deep and not safe to swim in as they had water snakes, but for someone who grew up in an area that was partly desert, I didn't believe the mumbo jumbo that the villagers did.

'Enough! We can't follow you anymore. It's either you tell us what we want or you will get it from me,' I said throwing a rock at him.

He stopped and swiftly turned towards us. His wooden face was in shadows as he had the moon to his back.

'I'm not the one who is to meet you. My master is,' he said in a voice I didn't recognise.

'Master? Who is your master and what does he want from me?' I asked.

'The master wants to know what this was doing in my wife's bag!' exclaimed a voice behind us that both Sidi and I knew well.

We turned in shock and found Abiyosa a few steps away from us. Supported by two bulky men was a figure that I could recognise even if I was in the underworld, Nwaluku.

He looked weak, tired and more like a person who had had one too many. There was a messy gash on his forehead and blood was flowing down his face in small rivers. His body was limp and the two guards who were always with Abiyosa let go of him and he tumbled to the ground groaning in pain.

'Nwaluku!' I cried out, running to him, but Abiyosa's hand closed over my wrist and twisted my arm painfully.

'And where do you think you are going you little witch? Where do you think you are going?' he asked again as he snarled like a rabid dog.

Dragging me across the sand, he threw me on the ground with force. I fell hard and felt my left wrist crack when I broke my fall with it. I winced in pain, but I was not going to scream. I was not going to give him the satisfaction. Sidi was frozen like a snow man on a hot day, numb with fear.

'What is this, my dear wife? What the hell is this, Thando?'

He shouted throwing a half-full packet of female condoms at me.

Oh oh! He knows, I thought to myself, fear gripping every muscle in my body.

'You are the one holding it so why don't you tell me what it is,' I shouted back. The lioness in me was slowly awakening. He let out an evil laugh and towered over me.

112

'Listen here, my girl. I am going to get the truth out of you if it's the last thing I do. I'm good at playing these games, sweetheart.

He traced my cheek with his finger and I turned my face away. As if that spelt disrespect, his palm connected with my face sending me sprawling on the sand. Nwaluku let out a moan that definitely was a cry for Abiyosa to let me go.

'Oh, look at what we have here. The proud father to be! Are you happy to have done the job for me, boy, huh?' he said, aiming his studded boot at Nwaluku. It connected with his ribs and I heard a crack. I felt as if my heart had been ripped out of me. Over and over again he aimed kicks at helpless Nwaluku who used his arms to try and avoid the boot. Gathering all the power I had, I picked up the knobkerrie Sidi had thrown to the ground and aimed it at Abiyosa, but one of his guards caught my hand in mid-air.

'Stop it, Abiyosa. Stop! I will tell you the truth. I will tell you,' I begged with tears streaming down my face.

My voice seemed to draw him out of his mad trance and he whirled around and faced me.

'Speak!'

'Yes, he is the father. Nwaluku is the father and I love him, Abiyosa. I love him so much. I have never loved you, never! You forced yourself on me, violated my life. Nwaluku cared and loved me. He is the father and not you. He not you, Abiyosa,' I spat out at him choking on my tears.

He smiled his white teeth glowing in the moonlight.

'You used these filthy things on me, opened that wretched hole for this thing. This boy I raised as my own son, one I clothed and fed. You surely proved what a worthless bitch you are. No wonder your father sold you in a heartbeat. You are a loose woman, Thando,' Abiyosa spat fire at me.

His words did not matter to me nor did they have any effect. If his ego was wounded then he had to swallow and take it like a man. As if he read my mind, he turned to Nwaluku.

'Now my boy, I'm going to teach you a lesson you will never forget. When you think of me, you will always remember Abiyosa. Always remember that a dog doesn't bite its master.'

Turning to his guards he gave an order I didn't expect.

'Drown him. He deserves to die!'

I don't know if some unknown force came over me, but as they dragged Nwaluku towards one of the deep pools, I ran after them and grabbed on to him.

'No, Abiyosa! No! Spare him. It was my fault. I'm the wrong one. I forced myself on him. I made him love me. Please listen to me. Nwaluku is innocent. Sidi, please tell him! Please, Sidi, tell him', I begged Abiyosa with my arms around Nwaluku.

My wretched husband laughed out loud like a crazy man.

'Oh my! Oh my, Thando. Now you know how to beg? Now you are pleading with me. For what? Your lover? You time is up, my beautiful flower'.

'I will do anything you want. Anything. Please let him go and I will be yours forever.'

'Anything, darling, you say?' he asked and I nodded vigorously.

'Thando, don't. You can't,' Sidi said, coming out of her shock zone.

'Oh, the puppet talks? We had missed you, Sidi, you betrayer,' Abiyosa said shooting the death stare at a terrified Sidi.

'You! Take this one away and keep her occupied if you know what I mean,' Abiyosa ordered his guard.

Oh no! Not Sidi. He couldn't possibly mean it. The guard picked a screaming and scratching Sidi up and got lost in the bushes. Her screams told me the story I could understand. He was raping her, violating my innocent Sidi, and it was all my fault.

'So, if I let your lover go, will you do anything I want?'

'Yes, I will. Anything.'

'Well then, cut it out. Get rid of the venom growing in your womb. It is growing in the womb meant for my heirs.'

He handed me a huge machete.

'What?'

'No, Thando, don't. He is going to kill me anyway. Don't do it,' Nwaluku shouted.

I slowly walked to Abiyosa and took the machete from him. I held it hovering over my abdomen and fixed my gaze on Nwaluku.

'I'm sorry, my love,' I said, raising the huge knife.

In swift movements I aimed it at Abiyosa, but he was too quick for me.

'You witch! You want to kill me? I will teach you a lesson you will never forget. Drown him NOW!'

The guard who held Nwaluku dragged him to the pond and forced him under water. A struggle broke out as Nwaluku fought to keep his head above water. His screams echoed in my ears in tune with the ones Sidi was letting out from behind the bushes. All the while Abiyosa held me tightly by the wrist, his evil laugh filling the air. I watched as the man I loved fought for his life. I watched as his strength became weak each and every passing moment until his body lay limp floating. The guard let go of his now still body and waded out of the water. Abiyosa let go of me and I ran and threw myself in the water.

'Nwaluku, Nwaluku, Nwaluku,' I wailed as pain shot through my body. I tried to pull him out the water, but strong hands pulled me back away from his body to the river bank.

'Enough of the drama now, Thando. You have performed enough; now it's time to go home. I warn you; you breathe a word to anyone and I will kill your family,' he said, spitting on my face.

The second guard came back dragging a sobbing Sidi and threw her in my arms.

Like prisoners, we marched through the bushes back to the Abiyosa plantation leaving Nwaluku's body floating aimlessly in the pool.

CHAPTER NINETEEN

A blood chilling wail broke through the air, sending birds on roost fluttering away. A second wail responded and my heart felt as if it had been ripped off me. I sat up from the grass mat and turned to the figure that was supposed to be lying next to me. The space there was empty and ice cold. Where could Sidi be?

After Abiyosa had brutally killed Nwaluku, he had taken us back to the compound, ordered us to our dwellings and told us never ever to speak of what had happened. I had sat all night crying my eyes out as I mourned the man who I loved. Sidi had just turned into a zombie and could not even say a word. Huddled together in the hut, we had mourned, wept, and screamed, but nothing could numb the pain that was eating our souls like some flesh-eating disease.

I rushed to the window and looked outside at the now-dawning sky. A crowd was gathering in the yard and my heart began to throb with more renewed pain. I thought that they had found my Lwuku, found his lifeless body. My heart was tearing into a thousand pieces. As if some invisible force was pulling me back, I battled to cover up and stepped outside the hut. Two of Abiyosa's goons readily came over to me and flanked me like bridesmaids.

'Remember what the master said or your family will be toast,' one whispered as I pushed my way through the small crowd that was gathered under a huge tree in the middle of the yard. As I made way, my eyes fell on Sadiku who was screaming and rolling on the ground like a possessed person. Some village women were trying to pacify her but in vain. I ran over to her, my heart pounding. She knows about Nwaluku I thought, fighting back tears.

'Move aside. Move aside and let me see Grandmother,' I said, putting an edge to a voice that was already trembling from all the supressed emotions. No one needed to be told twice. They made way for me and I knelt beside her. With care I cupped her face and looked deep into her eyes, but all I could see were two hollow pits that sadness had turned dark.

'What is it, Granny,' I customarily asked. Her hand rose as if she wanted to strike at me. I slowly followed the direction of her pointed finger until my eyes rested on what had caused all the commotion. My jaw dropped open, my heart stopped beating, and everything came to a standstill as if the clock master had switched off the main clock switch. Hanging from the huge Acacia tree, eyeballs turned inside out, and as cold as a fish, was Sidi. She had hanged herself.

'No!' I let out a blood-curdling scream as I looked into the hollow eyes that stared into the heavens in a very pitiful manner. I threw myself at the crowd of elders who were gathered close to the hanging body and yanked at the now cold legs. My body shook with pain, emotion and guilt. I had killed her. I had killed my own best friend. I kept on repeating the words in my head.

'Now child, you cannot be doing this when you are in this situation,' one woman said, pulling me back.

'Let me go. Let me go, please. Let me be with my Sidi. My Sidi. I want my Sidi back! Bring my Sidi back, aunt. Bring her back,' I sobbed, falling on my knees. The pain I had supressed in fear came out and now it was doubled. I was mourning two of the most important people in my life and all this was my fault. It was my fault, because I had always used Sidi and allowed her to aid in all my shenanigans; my fault, because I had set eyes on Nwaluku and fallen in love with him; my fault, because I was born a girl child in a family that saw me as a commodity. It was my fault because I had crossed Abiyosa too many times despite Sidi's warnings. All the ruined lives around me were my fault because of my ways.

The elders cut Sidi down and lay her stiff body on the ground. Like a mother who had just lost a child, I crawled to her and drew her head to my lap.

'I am sorry, so sorry I let you down, Sidi. Why? Why did you have to leave me, Sidi? Why am I so cursed this way?'

I screamed my head off, holding on to the cold body that was once a spirit of bubbly joy. Village women tried to pull me away, but I fought them like a mad lioness.

'Don't touch me! Are you happy now, huh? No one approved of my friendship with her and no one wanted her to help me around. Are you happy now? Here she is, DEAD! DEAD! DEAD! DEAD! Now go on. Beat the drums, pour some beer, kill a beast, and feast. Rejoice, for you have finally broken me.'

'My child, don't let grief take the better of you. Calm down,' one woman said, wrapping her arms around me. As if by instinct I collapsed into her arms and sobbed bitterly, clutching to her shirt for dear life.

As if my pain were not too much, two boys rushed in holding up a blood-soaked, torn shirt and gave it to Abiyosa. All this while he had been unmoving, just standing like a god and taking in the drama.

It was Nwaluku's shirt, tattered and torn and stained in blood. Sadiku took one look at it and the old woman lost it all. She crumbled into a heap unconscious.

'Ohhh! Ohhh! May the gods help us! *Ay Shangu* help us!' the woman cried.

'Sadiku, Sadiku. What is this I am seeing? What bad omen has befallen your house,' another exclaimed.

As if that was cue, wailing was set in motion and all around me women were crying and exclaiming, some shaking their heads and asking the gods why such a disaster had befallen the Abiyosa homestead.

My gaze shifted and fell on the one man I knew was the cause of this Armageddon. Abiyosa burrowed my face with his gaze, a smug, satisfied smile dancing on his lips. Oh Lord, if only I could kill him!

I walked towards one of the boys who had come bearing Nwaluku's shirt. I grabbed him by the throat.

'Where did you find that? Where on earth did you find that?' I asked while shaking him like the wind shakes the reeds in the river.

'Ahh, Sister Thando, I found it way down the canyon when I was following wounded prey that had broken from my trap. I was off following an impala track,' the now terrified boy answered, his bulgy eyes looking at me as if I was some kind of demon.

A hush fell over the place. Everyone stared at the boy who had come holding Nwaluku's tattered shirt. Abiyosa walked over to him and took the bloodied shirt from him.

'Son, did you say by the canyon? The same canyon that overlaps into the mashland?'

The boy nodded and slowly backed off from Abiyosa. This man had a presence that just set people off.

'Listen, everyone.'

His voice boomed over the silent congregation.

'It seems our beloved son has been devoured by the river masters. Only crocodiles can do this since the shirt was found near the canyon. This is surely a sad day for us. Two aspiring children lost to Mother Earth,' he said in a voice that seemed to be filled with remorse and could have made the Devil resign from Hell.

The nerve! Sadiku had come to and she was sobbing hysterically, calling out both Nwaluku's and Sidi's names, questioning the gods why they had taken her children away from her. My heart burned with pain, pain that ran through every vein in my body, palpating and crippling every part of my body. My Lwuku was gone and now Sidi too.

I had lost what I had called a family once upon a time, but now I had lost the rest of my world.

Sidi was buried like a queen, her grave dug next to the very tree on which she had taken her life. Questions unanswered hung in people's minds, questions that needed answers, yet no one could pinpoint that Abiyosa and I had the answers. As for Nwaluku, a special ceremony was done after Sidi was laid to rest. Abiyosa forbade me to attend as too much stress around me was unhealthy.

As my best friend was lowered into the earth, a part of me left with her. Who was going to fight off nasty village girls for me? Who was going to keep me company and put me on the straight and narrow if ever I strayed or laugh off cold winter nights with me? They say that one cries a river and I certainly did, but life had to go on and I had to find a new ally to get rid of Abiyosa.

Since no body was available for Nwaluku's burial, a *n'yanga* was called to perform some rites so that his soul would rest in peace. While all this was happening, Abiyosa put on a charade of a grieving father and uncle. He gave his Oscar performance such that I wondered if he really slept peacefully at night. This man was the Devil's step-brother for real and it was time for me to get even and take back all he had stolen from me.

I cried day and night. As days went by, I began to adjust to the absence of Sidi and Nwaluku. Sadiku had cut me off completely and whenever I would try to reach out she would just unleash her wrath on me. One particular day she almost skinned me alive. I had walked up to her hut and offered to grind the nuts for her. With eyes filled with hate she had given me her headmistress look.

'Hee! You have the nerve, *msidzana*! Help? You? Are you offering to help me? Haven't you helped enough around here, huh? Where is my Sidi? You let her die, didn't you? So much of a friend you are. What about my nephew Nwaluku, huh? You flashed your bosom for him day in day out and when I thought "No, this girl is well-mannered" what happens? You drive him to his death?' she fumed.

'No, Granny. No, I loved Nwaluku. I loved him so much, Granny.'

'Shut up, you wretched, cursed girl! I should never have allowed this fantasy of yours with my Nwaluku. Look how you drove him to insanity with your toxic love'.

Her words hurt more than the sting of a scorpion, yet I understood where she was coming from. I couldn't even bring myself to tell her the true identity of the child that was growing in my womb. I carried the burden and guilt with me, yet something still bothered me. Who was the hooded figure who had made sent me all those notes? I had to find out about this mysterious person. I really didn't have to look far before she presented herself before me.

One late afternoon as I was drowning in my sorrows and minding my own business as I had learned to do, one of Abiyosa's guards came to summon me. Of late Abiyosa had taken to calling me whenever he saw fit in order to insult me and humiliate me in front of his business associates. Seeing my humiliation gave him a boost in the balls and made him feel more of a man, I guess.

I dragged myself to his dwelling, half expecting that today was the day he would just put me out of my misery. As I neared the big hut he used for his private meetings, I heard jolly voices.

'At least he is in a good mood,' I thought as I announced my presence.

The laughter died down as he told me to enter. I scanned the room and saw a figure that I recognised instantly. It was the mysterious, hooded figure and from the chatter and laughter I had heard, this person was well acquainted with Abiyosa.

'Oh my wonderful, unfaithful wife is here! How many buckets of tears did you cry for that wretched imbecile?' Abiyosa asked, pointing to the mat that was in the far corner.

I clenched my fists into tight balls and took a deep breath. Breathe, Thando, breathe, I repeatedly told myself.

'I'm here. What do you want, Abiyosa?'

'Oh, I am shaking in my boots. Scary. I see you have got your mojo back, sweetheart'.

'What am I here for? Tell me.'

'Now, patience, darling, patience. I want you to meet the love of my life. The one who makes my heart beat like wild Massai drums. The woman who, despite being stuck with some spineless dog, bore me sons, sons I've always wanted,' he said with a satisfied smile on his face.

'You mean another woman? You mean to say I wasn't the one you loved most?' I asked in shock.

'Oh come on, don't act as if you cared much about that position. I gave you power and you spat in my face. I gave you status, but due to your strong rural animalistic upbringing you defied change and wealth. Did you really think I ever cared for you? Hahaha. I cared only for that wicked poison between your legs. Only that, you hear me?'

I raised my hand to strike him across the face, but my hand was caught in mid-air. I turned to find the hooded person standing beside me. The grip on my wrist tightened and funnily enough, there was something familiar about it.

'Let go of me! Who are you? Why did you kill my Lwuku?' I asked, kicking at the figure aimlessly.

Without warning my wrist was freed and I stumbled and landed hard on my buttocks. Laughter erupted from both of them and I fought back tears of fury.

'Let me introduce you to the most loyal woman of my life, the queen of my everyday dreams and the mother of my only son,' Abiyosa said, pulling off the hood that covered this mystery person.

As the huge cloth fell off, a flash of bright skirts caught my eye and I almost swallowed my tongue as I locked eyes with the person.

'Hello, Thandolwethu. I hope you missed me, step-daughter,' Aunt Paulina said, fixing me with her million dollar evil smile.

I was toast!

CHAPTER TWENTY

Our eyes locked like two bulls breathing down at each other at a rodeo. She had that smirking smile on her face and that victorious gleam in her eyes which I knew so well.

'Close that gaping hole of yours before you start catching flies,' she said, breaking the ice.

I stared and squared up to her.

'What the hell are you doing here?' I asked, charging at her like an enraged buffalo.

She side-stepped and I broke my fall with my outstretched arms which I had been intended to close around her neck.

'*Nci, nci, nci*. Still the feisty wild animal, I see,' she said, lovingly caressing Abiyosa.

I turned to him, my anger and fury fueled by this disgusting drama before me.

'You monster! What is all this? What is the meaning of all this, huh? What are you doing with this…, this witch?' I screamed at him.

He gave a tiny, cocky laugh.

'Oh my, you look more beautiful when you are angry. I wonder how that idiot boyfriend of yours managed to deal with you.'

'Don't you dare take his name! Don't you dare! I'm warning you, Abiyosa!'

'Oh? My dear Thando, your threats are nothing to me now. As long as big mama is here, I'm not worried or in need of your wasted body,' he said, mockingly.

They burst out laughing crazily.

'This, my dear unfaithful wife, is the love of my life, my jewel, my queen and the mother of my only son,' he said, looking at Paulina in a way that sent waves of jealously all over me.

He had never looked at me like that, yet here he was ogling Paulina as if she was some kind of delicacy.

One may wonder why I was jealous, but Abiyosa was still my husband be he a brute or not. Crazy isn't it?

'What? She is your what?'

'Oh, shut up! This is my place, Thando, not that run down, almost collapsing place your father owns', Paulina said.

Love? Mother of his son? This actually did not make sense. Paulina and the whole situation did not make sense. What was she doing here? Why was she this comfortable with Abiyosa?

'Wasn't getting me out of my father's house enough? Now you have followed me all the way to this place? Well, since you are here, when are you going back? Should I ask one of the herdboys to accompany you tomorrow morning?' I asked, putting my foot down.

Abiyosa and Paulina looked at each other and burst out laughing.

'It's more like when are you leaving this place, so I can spend more time with the father of my child,' she said.

It then dawned on me. My brother, Dumisani. He was Paulina's first son. Although most claimed that he looked like our great grandfather, now that I had got to know the situation, I could see the resemblance that he had to Abiyosa, being tall and heavily built.

Paulina did not waste much time to give me a crash course on her disgusting history. She and Abiyosa had been in an affair for years and my brother was a result of that affair. My father thought he had a son with her whereas she was secretly bringing up an illegitimate child in my father's house.

Abiyosa knew but his satisfaction could not be sated and when his frustration of not being able to be with his lover got to him, he came up with a plan to have me married off to him at all costs. It was more like "You bed the love of my life and I bed your precious daughter."

I gave a huge sigh of dismay.

'Now, now don't be sad, child. At least, I left that old cow called your mother sulking after me.'

I scampered into Sadiku's hut and found her packing her belongings.

'Grandmother, where are you going?' I asked, panic creeping into my every pore.

'My child, there is nothing left for me here. For years I've known the fact that Abiyosa loves Paulina. When the child was born, I delivered it with these hands of mine and I nursed that woman to health. So, child, she has come to her rightful place and I need to go,' she said stuffing clothes in a bag.

Abiyosa had abused Sadiku beyond her age. She could have left long back, but loyalty had stopped her. Oh! *Shangu* bless her soul. I sat staring as she busied herself, my thoughts running wild. If Paulina had something to do with my father losing his land to this man, then I was not going to take it lying down. If she thought that life would be rosy for her in the Abiyosa homestead, my homestead, I would show her wonders. I was Thando and I never backed down from a challenge, never.

'Hmm, I know that look, my child. Who are you planning to make your next victim?' Sadiku asked giving me a worried look.

'Don't worry, Granny. This fish is way bigger than you think. Let me handle it,' I said, leaving her hut for mine.

Life turned over with the arrival of Paulina. She threw her weight around and made sure we felt her presence. Abiyosa turned into a man I didn't know. He agreed to everything that Paulina wanted and everything was done her way.

One afternoon, Paulina went over her limits with Sadiku. Even though Sadiku still blamed me for Nwaluku's death, she was still an important part in my life and a relative to the child that was growing in my womb. Sadiku had been taking a rest under a huge tree when Paulina came up with a bucket of water and emptied it on her. The poor old woman was gasping for air and Paulina did not see anything wrong about it. I snapped.

'What do you think you are doing? Can't you see Granny is taking her afternoon nap,' I asked her furiously.

'Granny? You mean this witch was the reason I settled for your good-for-nothing father? All she does is sleep all day. If she wants to be here, then she has to earn her keep. No one is to stay for free. From today all of you will work for your wages,' Paulina shouted in her loud voice that had caught the attention of most of the homestead staff.

I had had enough of her and it was now time to teach her a lesson. Without warning, I threw a punch at her and it connected with her jaw.

'Ahh. What? How dare you hit me, you witch?'

'Well, this witch has had enough of you ordering us around. You abuse everyone and you are busy up and down with the man I married? What type of woman are you, aunt?' I asked, staring up at her.

'Haha husband? What husband rapes you instead of making love to you? Oh, you thought I didn't know? I know everything. You were just a sperm disposal pit while he awaited my return. Pity you didn't fall pregnant. And now you are with child for another man. Oh sorry, not another man, but a ghost, right? That Nwa... wat wat is now a ghost isn't he, or maybe an ancestor,' she said laughing scornfully.

As if some little demon awoke in me, I flew fists and all at her. How dare she talk about Nwaluku? No one would abuse Sadiku nor take the name of my late beloved Lwuku. She had opened a Pandora box and let its contents fly about. We looked at each other, screaming and ready to kill each other. Although I was pregnant, I still had my prowess as an African fighter. Paulina and I tore at each other like mountain lions over a tiny buck. This woman had been the source of my pain and now that she was in my house, she was going to respect me or I was ready to show her the highway.

A tiny crowd had gathered to watch a free wrestling match as we fought each other. Passersby had stopped and soon we had an audience. That fueled my strength and I gave her the beating of her life. Reaching over, I took Sadiku's walking stick and used it to cane an old woman. Hearing the screams that came from Paulina, one would swear she had never been caned as a child. The crowd cheered on as everyone knew what a monster she was.

'This is the last time you ever touch my Granny. If ever I catch you on Sadiku's case, I will do more than cane you. I will kill you, aunt,' I said, spitting on her.

The crowd cheered loudly as Paulina made her walk of shame. I felt good and like a hero, but that was to be short-lived.

Abiyosa got wind of the fight I had with Paulina and he was not pleased at all. As I had expected Paulina had told him a more drastic and modified version of the events and that had infuriated him. He came to my hut by night and barged in as if he were some soldier looking for a terrorist. Well I was a terrorist according to his new wife.

'Did you do it? Did you dare to hit my wife, Thando?' he asked, spit frothing from the corners of his lips like a dog mad on rabies.

'I did. So what? Your bitch should learn how to behave and know that this is my home,' I said, carelessly.

'Don't call her that. She is my wife and you will respect her and do as told. This is courtesy keeping you in this place, so don't act as if you own this place,' he said.

131

'What's keeping you from chasing me away then? Guilt? Or is it because you know what you did will come out, huh? That I would chirp like a bird and tell everyone that you are the murderer?'

That set him off and he came for me like a rodeo whip cracker.

'Today I will kill you, Thando. I will kill you.'

'What are you waiting for? Let's kill each other then, old man,' I said, drawing up a hoe stick I had hidden behind piles of sacks.

Without warning I whacked him hard on the head and followed by another blow to between his legs. He groaned in pain, but his eggs would not allow him to move.

'How is it, huh? You bully everyone and now you send this witch to do what? Take over my house? I never stopped you and your many women so you had no right to take my Lwuku away from me. So now we are even. You have brought this thing here and I am bringing Nwaluku's child,' I said, oozing confidence.

'This is not over, Thando,' he groaned in pain.

I knew my day would come, but for today I was ready to enjoy the little leverage I had over him. Chasing me away would mean the death of Sadiku and I knew even though Abiyosa was a monster, he would never do anything to hurt the unborn child I carried who was also a part of Sadiku.

Time flew like the wind and I began to show and get heavy with each moon that passed. Many times I would wonder what Sidi would have done seeing me this way. She would have been a good personal doctor for sure. Thoughts of her always flooded my mind and fueled my desire to revenge her death and that of Nwaluku, but it was not yet time. It was not yet time to execute what was way deep within the core of my thoughts.

One afternoon as I was out and about the river, searching for a fruit that I had grown fond of and craved due to the pregnancy, I felt a presence around me. It was the feeling that you get when you know you are being watched and followed. I stopped by some bushes and gathered fruit. That's when I heard it. A tiny soft yet croaky voice calling my name. I raised my head and looked around, but could not see anyone. Believing that my ears were playing tricks on me, I carried on with my fruit picking task. After a while I heard it again. It was a low whistle that sounded familiar. I stood up and scanned through the many bushes. Then I saw him, crouched behind a bush and waving to me with his hand. I beckoned him back, but he shook his head and indicated I follow him. My instinct told me to run for the hills, but I decided to follow him.

Abandoning the basket of fruit and the craving pangs, I hastily followed him deep into the bushes. I was wondering why he was here, why he was meeting me in the bushes and had not just walked up to the house, but you would never know with these healers. They did abnormal things. I followed him until we came to a quieter place that had tall trees around. I stopped a few feet from this respectable village healer.

'Makhosi. Why did you call me here?' I asked.

'Shh! Not so loud, my child. Not so loud *ngane yami*,' he said his voice full of uncertainty.

I had heard stories from Sidi that this particular healer would approach a person at odd places if he had something to tell them and I had never thought it would happen to me. I guess my stunts and antics had spread all around about the crazy, pregnant woman.

'Makhosi, why am I here? Does my elder need me to help him with something? I'm sorry, but I cannot touch all the funny stuff you healers use,' I said.

'Your sharp tongue is the source of your powers, my child, yet you do not know how to control it.'

'Hoo, stop there, old man, what powers? If you need an apprentice, then you barked up the wrong tree.'

'I wouldn't dare, child, even if you were the last person in the universe. I would die from that sharp tongue of yours before I could teach you anything,' he said in a light tone more like a chuckle. He was teasing.

'Sit down, my child,' he said, as he leaned on a tree.

I sat few feet from him and I gave him my inquisitive look. He cleared his throat and spoke.

'A few years ago a young girl and her brother lodged at my sister's hut on their way to this area. That young girl was you. My sister felt something about you and when she passed on, she told me to look for the girl who had come to her hut and offer her my help. Do you happen to follow what I am saying?'

My mind did a race-over trip to the day I had left my home to go to the Abiyosa plantation. The old woman who had given us shelter had forced something in my hand which I had forgotten about. I had forgotten about her, but now that the old man was talking about her, everything came back in a flash.

'If you still have what she gave you, child, it is time to use it now,' he said, fixing his black eyes on mine.

CHAPTER TWENTY-ONE

I stared aghast at him, my mind doing math of its own. As much as the aura around this healer gave me good vibes I was still sceptical about trusting him. Unlike my late friend Sidi, who saw the good in everyone, I always had the inner voice telling me another story.

'Your hesitation and that volcanic thought race in your mind is a waste of time. I want what you want more than anything. Unfortunately, my gift prevents me from touching that wretched animal, but you my child are a gift from the gods.'

'Old man. Are you working for my step-mother? Are you on Abiyosa's payroll?' I asked my voice cracking.

'No, child. If I were, how would I know about what lies within the secrets of your heart?' he asked.

Yes, that made sense. He was truly a messenger of the gods and whatever his agenda was, I did not care as long as it brought us together and towards our main goal, getting Abiyosa. He had been a terror, but enough was enough. As one would guess, it was not going to be a walk in the park to get Abiyosa. First of all, he had people around him all the time and whatever healer he went to was strong. What bothered me a lot was getting caught. If he ever got wind of me meeting this healer, I would be a good as dead.

'Child, go home, take what lies within your belongings and bring it to me,' he said in a croaky voice.

Without any further words, he left.

I made haste back to the compound, excitement putting a spring to my step such that the life that was growing within me juggled up and down like circus balls. Finally I had pinpointed a person that Abiyosa would not suspect, someone who was ready to help me. As I approached the hut I now shared with Sadiku, I was met by a sick sight. Guards were moving my belongings from the hut and ferrying them to a much smaller one, a lodge isolated at the end of the yard.

'What are you doing? Who gave you permission to touch my belongings? How dare you?' I frantically screamed.

One of the guards told me that Paulina had ordered that the hut be cleared for her own use and henceforth I was to occupy a much smaller hut.

I rummaged through all my belongings, searching for a small box in which I had kept my little treasure.

'Looking for this,' Paulina's voice said from behind me. I turned and found her dangling the box I was searching for under my nose.

'Give me that! How dare you touch my things without my permission?'

'I didn't know I had to ask. This is my home and anything within these grounds belongs to me,' she said smugly.

I gave her my most cool look as I took a step closer to her. I came level to her ears.

'Listen to me carefully, Paupau. If you know what's good for you, you will give me back what belongs to me or else,' I whispered firmly to her.

'Or else what, huh? You think you can do anything to me now?'

'Or else I will go to that bush by the kraal. You know I am allergic to the vine over there and we both know who uses that vine to ward off ants from her flowers, isnt? What do you think Abiyosa will say when I cry wolf and say you came with the vine and you rubbed it on my arms? Hmm, let me see, he is still my husband and cares for me despite everything. So, if I say you wanted to kill me with the vine, guess what woman he will believe?' I said, giving her a wink.

That worked for she thrust the box at me and walked away. Yes, I had got her for now, but phase one of my plans for revenge was not yet in motion.

With the daintiness of a fairy, I got to work after Paulina had gone. You may think that I was foolish to succumb to her demands, but I wasn't. Paulina wanted a good meal to be cooked by me and pass it off as hers. She was going to get much more than she had bargained for. Difficult as it was to ground the peanuts, I slaved over the grinding stone until I had a very good measure of peanut butter. I added it to the already ripe pumpkin leaves and the aroma that rose from the pot brought forth the bent-over figure of Sadiku.

'My child, you should not be doing such heavy work. That's not good for the baby,' she said, taking the wooden spoon from me.

'It's no trouble, Granny. A pregnant woman needs to exercise, right?'

'Oh, may the gods strike that wicked snake down. I have never seen such madness in my life. Now, take this relish pit and put it inside. I will take care of the mealie porridge, my child,' she said, handing me the steaming pot.

Given the chance, this was the time for me to get my phase one into motion. On entering the hut, I carefully put the pot down and crept to the door to check on Sadiku. She was busy with the mealie porridge. Fumbling within the cave between my breasts, I took out a ball of powder. Yes, you guessed right. This was part of the contents that lay within the safety of the tiny box that Paulina almost discovered. With much care, I emptied the powder into the relish pot, after dishing out my share of course. I wasn't going to let such good food go to waste. Stirring gently, I mixed the powder into the peanut butter goulash and then dished out some for my dear husband and my precious aunt. Now I had to wait for the fireworks to begin and I just couldn't wait.

Nightfall came slowly. I was so impatient for Abiyosa and Paulina to come back that I tossed and turned my mat. The sound of the car stopping sent my baby jumping vigorously. Tenderly, I ran my hand over my huge tummy. My Nwaluku was growing strong. It was the only bond left of what was our love, the only flame that still flickered with life through all the rough nights I was having. A loud knock broke into my intimate moment with my unborn child. Madam Paulina was back!

'Okay, there is no need to break down the door, you crazy woman,' I said, opening the door just a little crack.

'Did you cook the food? Is it just the way he likes it?' she whispered.

'Why are you whispering, aunt? Speak louder,' I said, raising my voice so that Abiyosa who was just a few yards away could hear. If she could scold me loudly for the world to hear, why not speak loudly so that her so-called hero would know that I had done all the work.

'Shh, not so loud. Where is the food?' she whispered back, trying to force the door open.

'In your room, aunt. I left it near the fireplace. They are probably still warm,' I said, raising my voice a little bit higher to catch Abiyosa's attention.

Paulina slammed the door in my face and hurried off cursing. I chuckled to myself as I retired to my blankets.

It was a matter of time before the drama erupted in Abiyosa's hut. It was game on for dear Paupau.

Loud shouts erupted in the middle of the night. I woke up from my dazed stupor and sat up. I let out what one would call a wicked sleepy laugh. The drama had started in Abiyosa's hut. Gingerly, I went to the door and opened it just a few inches. I could see Sadiku in her doorway too. Guess I was not the only one who had heard the noise.

'What is all this, Abiyosa? Oh Great gods! Are you trying to kill me now,' Paulina's voice came loud and clear from the hut.

Abiyosa's distinct deep voice could be heard trying to pacify her.

'Don't touch me right now! What has happened to you? What is all this? Oh, my goodness.'

'Please keep it down. Do you want to wake up everyone in this compound?' Abiyosa said, raising his voice.

'Yes, let them wake up and see what I'm seeing. What is all this? How can your manhood vanish just like this from a huge rod to a small pinky? What type of voodoo are you playing on me?' Paulina shouted.

I couldn't hold back my laughter and I just crumbled by the door and laughed hysterically. If she thought this was weird, wait until I got to phase two with her. I still had more of the powder and I was well bent on giving these two a taste of their own medicine. Phase one was to create conflicts between them until they drove each other insane. This was just an introduction of what phase one was and already my loving doting aunt was freaking out. I got back into the room and crawled back into my blankets. The muti worked faster than I had thought. First it was to affect Abiyosa by shrinking his prized manhood close to invisibility each time he tried to get intimate with Paulina and what was to happen secondly was yet to be discovered by Paulina herself. I just couldn't wait to drive her insane. These two had messed with the wrong pregnant cougar.

CHAPTER TWENTY-TWO

Morning came and the sun kissed the earth with tenderness. Birds chirped in jolly song and I sat in my room a very weird yet satisfied smile on my face. I just couldn't shake off the sound of the uproar that Paulina and Abiyosa had caused the previous night. Oh *Shango* forgive me! If only I could have been a fly in their hut and seen the drama live. I gingerly made up my sleeping mat and folded my blankets. I knew Aunt Paulina would be in a foul mood and I just couldn't wait to rub her up the wrong side and add a little bit of salt and pepper to the wound. Yes, why not? By now everyone knows that I am a very talented opportunist don't they?

I poured cold water from the basin and started my morning ritual. Whoever said humans should bathe and especially the one who fabricated this so-called myth that a woman should use cold water to bathe so as to be strong and actually not transfer laziness to her man, must have had a special brand of weed. This was pure nonsense to me. I was to deal with the important areas of my body and then do the rest late in the day. I mean what's more important than a dash by the armpits, face and the velvet cake? As I always said to Sidi (Oh bless her poor sweet soul) dry wash in the morning and then wet wash when it's warm enough.

Sadiku always thought I was one filthy person, but what did she expect? I grew up with boys. Unfortunately, with my little ninja growing within me, I was taking the wet wash every single morning and instead of running half a mile I had to wash thoroughly. I finished my morning ritual and stepped outside. The warmth of the sun on my skin felt velvety like a lover's kiss and the cool breeze sent little

Nwaluku kicking up a storm. Automatically, I ran my hands over my now bulging tummy. In a matter of time, I would be holding my child in my arms, yet not with her father I thought sadly.

'Hey, you lazy thing! No hot water was sent to my room this morning. Is this the time to wake up,' a voice I knew well said from across the yard.

I looked over at grumpy Paulina walking towards me. Oh my, the frustration of a woman who couldn't give coitus to her man.

'Who died and made me your personal maid, aunt? Last time I checked both you and I are brides in this yard. No, I mean, I AM THE BRIDE IN THIS YARD! And you are what? Small house, middle house or just another of Abiyosa's many whores,' I shot back.

'Oh, really? Well that idiot Sidi died and now you have to take whatever duty she had to do for me!'

'You dare not! You dare not talk about Sidi or I will...'

'Hit me again? Haha, now I'm ready for you. Be careful you might end up pissing that monster growing within you,' she said a satisfied smile on her face.

I took a calm deep breath before I answered her.

'You know, aunt, they say an unfed bitch usually takes its frustrations out on its puppies. I mean it's not my fault that everyone here knows that last night you didn't get some probing in that mine of yours, but who can blame him. Some fields are just too big to play on,' I said, turning on my heels and heading towards Sadiku's hut.

What I felt was the thud close to my feet. Poor Paulina had thrown a broom at me in anger. If she thought she was going to push me around, she had another think coming.

The tension between Abiyosa and Paulina over the nocturnal activities seemed to overflow for the meals for the day Abiyosa requested that they should be prepared in my kitchen. That made aunt fume like a bloated bullfrog, but there was nothing she could do. I guess poor Abiyosa was angry that he had failed to satisfy his woman and had to endure her wrath and humiliation. He should have asked my father before he brought the she-devil home. With the joys of a virgin, I helped Sadiku prepare every meal. Aunt criticized and complained about the meals, but I was not yet done with her. I had to make a plan to get Abiyosa to be calm and happy and to actually drive aunt up the wall.

It was while she was sitting under the shade of the huge Acacia tree with Abiyosa, both in deathly silence, that I approached with a gourd full of amarula drink. I knew Abiyosa had a weakness for that particular drink. Upon reaching them I curtsied a little.

'My husband, it's a hot day so I thought I should bring you some refreshment,' I said in my makoti voice.

Abiyosa looked up in shock, but a small smile danced on in lips.

'Thank you, Thando. I see you have learnt your lesson well,' he said, taking the gourd from me.

Phew! Learnt a lesson? This man did not know me well.

'What poison have you put for him? You want to kill him?' aunt asked, pointing at me.

'Enough! At least this girl has the respect to talk to me politely,' Abiyosa shouted at her.

Aunt's face turned ashen like that of a ghost and, oh boy, did I feel good inside.

'But Abi, this thing... '

'This thing is still my wife. Why can't you understand that? For once can you just shut up!' Abiyosa said, getting on his feet and walking away.

He paused and turned back.

'Thando, bring food to my hut. I would appreciate your company, too,' he said, walking off.

The look on Paulina's face was worth its weight in gold. If looks could kill, then I would've died that very moment.

'You heard him. He wants my company, aunt. Maybe he is too tired of that sharp tongue of yours or maybe it's your fanged velvet cake that has chased him away,' I said, laughing my way back to my hut.

Phase two had just begun. Divide and conquer.

Paulina's had overstayed her welcome in my home and it was time she packed her rags and hit the road, but how? That was the difficult part. I was supposed to pull a huge trick from the hat to make Abiyosa kick her out. I kept feeding the divide and conquer medicine to both of them and it was working wonders, but not to my liking. I wanted her out and out for good.

One evening I gave Paulina an overdose in her favourite nightcap cup of tea and what had transpired that night had sent unborn Lwuku kicking a storm. Apparently, instead of Abiyosa's huge shaft sliding smoothly into her velvet cake, he found it tightly closed. It was much tighter than a newborn. Oh boy! The fight they had had; each accusing the other of using muthi and all sorts of things. The fight had ended with Abiyosa knocking on my door asking if he could spend the night. As much as I hated this rogue, I played along, happy within that my prey was delivering itself on a silver platter. It was time to get my plan to remove Paulina from the homestead in motion.

It was late in the afternoon that a crash was heard coming from Abiyosa's hut. Loud screams of agony from Paulina could be heard against the din of the many goat kids that were running all over the yard. I pulled myself up and walked toward Abiyosa's hut. I met Sadiku on her way there too.

'What's going on, Grandmother? What is all this noise about?' I asked.

'How will I know, child. Let's get closer and hear why these two are at it again,' she said, shuffling her feet.

'You witch! You are a witch, Paulina, hee!' Abiyosa said.

'I swear I know nothing of this. I don't know how all this got into my bag and how all this is here. I swear, my love, I would never do such a thing, never,' Paulina pleaded, tears falling.

'No, Paulina. You have gone too far. You know I don't want anything to do with all that voodoo stuff, but to bring this here? No! You need to go.'

Yes! My lovely plan had worked. Abiyosa was angry and he was ready to kick Paulina out. As we got to the door, we found him holding a small bag that was filled with all

146

sorts of weird stuff from dry chicken legs to some tiny roots and shiny stones. There was also some powder in a tin which had a paper on it. When asked to open it, Paulina was hesitant, claiming she was afraid, but a slap from Abiyosa sent her flying. A tiny paper fell out and Abiyosa's name was written on it. That sent him over the edge. He half-dragged and half-lifted her towards the gate.

This was what I had wanted, for Paulina to be gone, but it was not my entire plan.

'My husband, please. Please don't do this to her,' I pleaded, stepping in front of Abiyosa and a weeping Paulina.

'What?' they both asked in unison, looking at me as though I was crazy.

Yes, this is what I wanted.

'Please don't send aunt away. Please. She is the only link I have to my old life. Forgive her on my behalf. Understand that she felt I was taking your love. That's why she had to mark her territory. Please love her for the sake of your love for me. I promise that after the baby is born, I will honor and respect you,' I blabbered mindlessly.

Abiyosa seemed to calm at the soothing voice I used on him. My crocodile tears got to him and he calmed down.

'If it weren't for this girl, I swear...Stay away from me, witch!' he said, storming off with Sadiku hot on his heels, leaving a hysterical Paulina in a heap on the ground.

I looked at the pitiful sight before me and felt disgusted. I walked over to her and sat next to her.

'Now you are at my mercy, love. Now you are at Thando's mercy. Now I own you, aunt,' I whispered softly.

Paulina gave me a look of disbelief.

'You, you, you... ' she stammered.

'Shh! Silence! Now you dance to my music,' I said, getting up.

I had Paulina where I wanted her.

CHAPTER TWENTY-THREE

'Did you fall out of your mother's womb when you were a little baby?' Sadiku asked, giving me one of her "You better tell me what you are up to" looks.

The poor old lady was aghast with shock at what I had just done. Who in their right mind would let go of such an opportunity to have their competition taken out? I had every chance to get Aunt Paulina out in a jiffy, but then that would have made my victory short-lived and I still needed her to dance to my tune. She was the main key to what I had in store for dear, caring Abiyosa.

'No, Grandmother. I'm as alert as a doe after giving birth. Aunt is here because of me now. She is at my mercy, no at our mercy, because I can't forget what she has done to us. No one touches my mother-in-law and gets away with it,' I said, a distant look clouding my ever brown eyes.

'Did you just call me your mother-in-law?' old Sadiku asked, disbelief evident in her voice.

'No, I meant the goat behind you. Of course you are my mother-in-law. You nurtured Nwaluku, so to me you are my mother too, but don't get too used to it. This sentimental love only lasts for few minutes,' I said, giving her an affectionate hug.

She hugged me back and I felt the overwhelming motherly love I had so much wished to get from her, flow throughout my body. At times like this I felt sad and alone. My mother was now a memory to me, my father a phantom that I did not wish to think of. What had happened to my perfect life? What had happened to the doting parents that used to love me more than life itself? Both had become a thing of the past, just fading memories that kept probing at my subconscious. Parents are meant to love us and protect us, but mine chose to sell me. They sold me to an old fox that not only made my life living hell but also took a part of me and sent it to the land of skulls. Sadiku pulled back from the embrace and stared at me. Tears were rolling down my cheeks aimlessly.

'Now, child, this is not the time to shed tears. This is not the time to look weak. A tiny victory over your aunt doesn't mean the storm is over. More is yet to come and you know she won't take this lying down,' she said, taking one of her many shawls and wiping tears off my face.

'Grandmother, this is a moment I should be sharing with my mother. I should await my first child under her guidance, but look at me now, neither parents nor siblings.'

'No child. You have me. I will guide you in every way and I will make sure nothing happens that will cause harm to you or the baby. You are my children,' she said.

Sadiku had really changed and if it had not been for her, I would have gone totally insane. There were days I missed Sidi a lot, her laugh and crazy antics, but no one could understand the empty void I felt at missing my family. My brothers would be courting girls at this time of the year, some getting the cattle ready for the planting season. My aunts would either be pregnant or busying themselves with grain selecting for the ploughing days. Father would be pacing the yard like a caged tiger, trying to come up with the best solution for his cattle. And I, being the favourite, would be given the babysitter task. Such had been my life but all this was now a distant memory.

'Don't overthink, child. You have had rough times, but I swear all will be well soon,' Sadiku said and broke my line of thought.

'I know, Granny. All shall be well,' I said, pulling myself up. 'I want to take a walk to the river. I will be back soon.'

I excused myself and took the path that led to the river.

I walked the now-green, carpeted route to the river. The early rains had turned the smoky grey yellow bushes to spits of dark green. The path looked like a picture from some imaginary story. I walked slowly fighting a never-ending battle with my thoughts. There was so much I wanted to do. At the same time, my hands felt as if an invisible cord tied them together. I don't know why I was going to the river, but deep within me I felt a strong feeling that I was to see the old healer once again. After I had met him for the first time, he just vanished like a puff of smoke and no matter how many times I went to the river, I never got to see him. Amazingly, I searched endlessly for his hut, but never found it. It seemed as if I had conjured him out of my mind. I got to the river bank and plopped down on the cool sand. There was a deathly silence around and the birds seemed to have taken a break from singing. I drew patterns in the sand with my toe. Repeatedly, all I could write was Nwaluku's name.

'Sadness always brings me to you,' a voice sad beside me.

I jumped up terrified because I thought I was alone.

'For God's sake, will you stop? You almost gave me a heart attack, old man,' I said, staring into the bloodshot eyes of the healer who had suddenly appeared beside me like a ghost.

'Sorry, child. Ancestors send me wherever I have to go. You look troubled a lot today,' he said, putting his animal skin bag down.

'Yes, Makhosi. I'm very restless a lot. I feel as if there is a spirit that follows me. Like someone who is close and dear to me is always watching me. Makhosi, I feel Nwaluku everywhere, as if he is still with us. I know I sound like a mad woman, but this is how feel, Makhosi.'

'What if what you feel is right?' he asked quietly, fixing me with his penetrating gaze.

'What do you mean? Old man, you have started with your crazy talk again. Your riddles baffle me and instead of putting me at ease you always leave me more stressed and confused,' I said, anger and irritation creeping into my voice.

'It is your anger that has always kept him away. Your anger has always hindered him to complete his mission. It is that anger that has kept the big fire raging between the two of you,' he said, fixing his gaze at the deep pool before us.

'Oh my goodness! Makhosi, I really don't know if your ancestors can give straight messages, but right now they are starting to rub me up the wall. Who are you talking about and what do you mean? Can you just speak without being as dramatic as a stage actor?' My fury was starting to build up.

'Calm down, child. All in good time. Not now and not yet. It's very risky to do things under the glare of light.'

'Oh! So you mean I should come back here when all the witches of this area are roaming around on hyenas backs? Not a chance, *madala*.'

'You are a very stubborn child. I'm glad I never got to be your grandfather. See you at midnight,' he said picking up his bag and shuffling away like a snail.

I stared at his hunched back. This haggy man had really started to freak me out, yet I felt a sense of trust in him and security. Picking myself up, I left for home as the sun started to kiss the tree tops in its reddish glare.

Have you ever tried to catch sleep when knowing that something big was about to go down? Imagine how I felt. I was like a newly appointed soldier on the night before being sent to battle. My nerves were all over the place and I tossed and turned.

'Will you please stop tossing like a donkey taking a sand bath? My goodness how can one sleep?' Sadiku croaked sleepily from her mat across the heart.

'Sorry, Grandmother. Maybe you should just sleep in your hut tonight,' I said, taking a chance with her.

'You don't have to ask twice, my child. Maybe I will be able to sleep tonight,' she said, getting off her mat.

When she got to the door she paused.

'Do get some sleep; you need to rest,' she said, shutting the door behind her.

Phew! Finally she was gone. Not that I hated sharing the hut with her, but tonight I needed to do my ninja sneak out without her asking me a lot of questions. I looked at my clock and it read 10 p.m. Time to go.

I quickly pulled a dress over the nightdress I had on and threw a blanket over my shoulders to keep the cold at bay. Stealthily, I made my way out of the yard, first bribing the dogs with some leftover meat that I had kept aside. These dogs had the tendency to bark endlessly until people woke up. I made my way towards the river, my heart pounding like sangoma drums. I felt so nervous and afraid, yet curious at the same time. What did the old man have in store for me? The same sense of uneasiness I had had earlier seemed to return again, this time strongly. I felt my unborn child kick vigorously. He was excited too.

I got to the river and I was relieved to see the healer's hooded figure sitting at the far side of the bank. The moon was shining brightly and it cast ghostly shadows.

'You came?' he said quietly.

'Yes, Makhosi. I wouldn't miss your voodoo for the world.'

He shook his head slowly and busied himself with the contents of his bag. I sat staring at the gleaming dark waters of the pool, my mind abuzz with many questions. Was I normal or just plain stupid? I was trusting a disappearing old man with my life and that of my unborn baby, What if he was some kind of ritualist who needed body parts of a pregnant woman to create his spells and magic? What if I was just a meal for his pack of hyenas? A hyena laughed in the distance and I froze. Oh my, I was a goner. This man was surely going to feed me to his hyenas.

'Such thoughts usually send people into a mad state. You will drive yourself into madness by having such a very imaginative mind. Who told you ritualists keep hyenas?' he asked calmly.

Damn it! He can read minds too.

'I was not thinking of such, Makhosi. I, I, …' Words failed me.

'Save it, child. It is time now. Get up,' he said, pulling me to my feet.

'Time for what, Makhosi?' I asked, fear creeping into my voice making it hard to speak.

'Your thoughts and the desire and sorrow in your heart brought me back today. The great ones have spoken and you have unbound the chains that have kept me at bay. It is time now, Thando. Time to use your given gift.'

'What gift, Makhosi? I asked, confusion zigzagging through my mind.

'The woman you met on your way to this place, the woman who said you are the chosen one, was not bluffing. You have to admit to yourself that you have a calling. Ask yourself why the bull at your home never attacked you when you were younger? Why did it maul over your brothers but made a U-turn when it came close to you?'

'How do you know about that? I have never told anyone about it, not even Sidi?'

'I know all, child.'

That shook me. I had almost forgotten the time when I was just a ten-year-old and one of the bulls had gone on a crazy rant and chased us around the field. When it had got to me, it had just decided to go on its way and left me unharmed and my brothers nursing many bruises. I had never read much into the incident at that time, but now it was starting to worry me.

'It is time, dear. It is time for you to unchain him,' he said, standing up and walking to the edge of the pool. I followed him and stood shivering slightly by his side.

'Open out your mind and call out to your love. You thoughts will either be his victory or his doom. It is in your hands whether you want the river gods to release Nwaluku or not. He has been kept *ithwasa* for so long. Unchain him, child,' he said in a voice unlike his.

'Nwaluku? Is this some kind of joke, old man?' I asked, fury building up.

'You have no time to waste, Thando. Use your love to bring him back. Look at the water,' he said firmly.

I shifted my gaze to the water which from nowhere had started to bubble as if an invisible fire was heating it up.

'Think about all the good things about him. Hurry, we have little time.'

Scared as I was, I focused on the bubbling pool and focused my energy and that of my unborn baby in thinking about all the good that Nwaluku was.

CHAPTER TWENTYFOUR

I willed myself to focus though it was proving to be a task. The waters of the pool bubbled like the *pre sgodokhaya* soft porridge and a gust of strong wind blew water into our faces. The air turned massively cold as if by some invisible force the old man had conjured up some snow. I kept my eyes glued to the bubbles which grew bigger and bigger.

'You are almost there, child. Do not let him go. He has been kept away from us for far too long.'

If I had an extra hand, I would have smacked the old man hard on his bald head. Did he really think I was not focused well enough? I was putting all my toes and intestines in all the focus I could muster, yet he kept coaxing me to focus.

'I am. Just stop pushing me,' I said through gritted teeth.

Slowly the wind around us began to subside although the waters of the pool kept swirling as if some invisible hand were stirring them up. I saw a flash of white appear on the surface and the much recognisable plumage of ostrich feathers broke the water. A figure slowly emerged from the waters. I strained my eyes against the mist that had enveloped us, but all I could see was the much recognisable headdress that the sangomas connected to the water spirit wore. As much as I tried to focus, I could not make out the face of this person.

'It is done now. You may take a breather,' the sangoma said, moving towards the now calmer water and the now half-submerged person. I sank to the ground in exhaustion, breathing heavily like a steam engine. My child was giving wild kicks like a female warding off a male ready to mate.

'Makhosi! *Nyandezulu! Nhliziyo yeNjuzi*!,' the sangoma said to the figure that stood head bowed. I watched silently as the sangoma took out his horse tail staff and swished it around the figure, chanting incantations and praiseful words.

'Come, child. Only you have the power and right to perform this last rite with him,' he said calling me over to the swirling waters.

With him? Who was he? If this old man thought I was going to freeze my ass in the cold water, he had another think coming. I had obliged to come and do whatever rite he wanted me to do, but I was not putting myself in cold water.

'Makhosi, you want me to get into the pool? I can't even swim. I will drown before I can even reach that.' I said, pointing to the still figure in the middle of the pool.

'Make haste! We are losing the cover of darkness. You need to complete this ritual so that the spirit of Nwaluku can come back to us. What you see right before you is only the body. You need to bring his spirit back and only you can do this, Thandolwethu.'

Reluctantly, I stepped into the cold, icy water and waded up to my waist to the still rigid figure.

'Now child, put your arms around him and whatever happens do not let go or close your eyes. It is all up to you to free his spirit and bring him back to us,' the old man said.

I wrapped my arms around him and held on tightly. The sangoma began to chant incantations; his voice rising up until it was now more like a war cry. The water began to ripple as if something was moving swiftly underneath. I kept repeating to myself not to close my eyes even though my normal instinct willed me to do so. Something slimy began to crawl up my back. It felt huge and super cold. It climbed up my back until I felt something flat rest at the top of my head. I dared not tilt my head up, but from my sensory nerves I could tell that this was one of my worst fears. A loud hiss echoed right above me and I just froze.

A huge snake wound its body around both of us and try as I might, I found myself unable to shut my eyes. Coil by coil, it wrapped itself around us. The water began to warm up around us and all sounds were drowned by the thunder and rumbling that seemed to come from within the depths of the pool. The snake sent gallons of spit all over us and all I could think of was that this monster is salivating before having me for a snack. After what seemed like an endless shower of spit, I felt the snake unwrap itself and slowly slither away into the pool. The wind dropped and the rumbling became quieter. The old man waded into the pool and set us apart.

'Submerge yourself, my child, and wash. Then turn and go. Take the path that leads to my hut and wait for me there.'

'But, Makhosi, who is this and... '

'Enough, child! Do as I say, he urged in his most dismissive way.

I took a dip and washed as much as I could. My huge bulging tummy was a torrent of kicks. After the much-needed, yet cold bath, I followed the path that led to the healer's hut. What did he mean when he had asked me to use all my memories of Nwaluku? Was it possible that this person I had helped become initiated was somehow linked to my now gone Lwuku? Question after question racked my brain, but to no avail. Upon reaching the hut, I gladly welcomed the warmth and sanctuary that it offered. A few minutes later, the door burst open and I scampered to my feet. The healer entered and right at his heel was the one person I never thought I would ever see again, Nwaluku!

He was decked in all the splendour and glamour of a newly qualified sangoma. He had an array of colourful beads made into bracelets and anklets adorning his wrists and ankles. A huge animal skin covered him with a much larger bead belt fitted to his waist. Cutting from one shoulder across his chest to his waist was a snake skin that glowed darkly in the glare of the fire that warmed the hut. His headdress made him look much taller than I could remember. I searched his eyes, but all I saw was a far distant and stern look.

Will he recognise me? I wondered, nerves threatening to wrack my brains apart. What if he had no idea who I was? What if all memories of our life together were lost to him? What if wherever he had been, they had made him forget his past life in preparation for his future?

All these questions flooded me and I felt woozy. As I swooned over, his strong, muscular arms caught me.

'You will do no such thing, Thando! You will not faint on me,' a voice I had long yearned to hear said close to my ear.

I looked up into the warming eyes of Nwaluku.

'Lwuku, is that you? Where have you been? Why did you leave us? Why did you go away?'

I shot questions at him one after the other.

'Child, calm down. Your frantic questions are not good for your health especially when you are with child,' the sangoma said.

'Oh, Makhosi! Yet you let me swim in cold water. I want to know where he has been and why you didn't you tell me the truth from the first time I met you.'

'Child, sit and I will tell you what happened to let me and this now-new sangoma meet,' he said in his always collected voice.

He was much better than Sadiku at handling my rants. He kindled the flames back to life and a much brighter glow filled the hut. Nwaluku helped me to a heap of mats and wrapped a blanket round my shoulders. He sat beside me and held my hand tenderly. After clearing his voice, the sangoma spoke.

'It was on one early morning when I was out about looking for my healing herbs when I felt a great urge that there was a presence at the river. I had ignored this urge and after collecting all my needed herbs, I had left for home. That night I didn't get any sleep, but I kept seeing a shadow in my dreams, a shadow that didn't materialised into form. Night after night I had the same dream. Finally, I decided to consult the great ones about this one dream that bothered me. That's when I was directed to the very same river. When I got there, I felt this young man's spirit although it was very week.

That very same pool we were at, to mere folk, it's just a deep pool rumoured to house a snake, but to us, the servants of the ancestors, it is the sacred place of the *Injuzi*. I had got to the pool and consulted. That is when I discovered that when he was dumped in this pool, the spirits of the pool had pulled him under and he had been kept under their guidance as *Ithwasa*. As per norm, when a person happens to fall under the spell of the *injizi* spirits, if his family members mourn him, the spirits get angered and they kill the person. With Nwaluku, it was a different case. You mourned him as someone who had been drowned and later mauled by wild animals, hence pity was taken upon him and he stayed with the spirits until today. The ancestors guided me to you for I was shown that you were of pure soul and held an important key to this young man's life. That is why our paths crossed, child.'

'But Makhosi, why didn't you tell me? Why didn't you put me out of my misery?' I asked, tears rolling down my cheeks.

Nwaluku wiped them off with his hand.

'You know, child, how much of a loose cannon you can be. It was not yet the right time to trust you with such a huge matter. I needed to establish my trust in you,'

'So what now, Makhosi? What is to happen,' I asked, my voice filled with hope.

I could already see Abiyosa's face at seeing Nwaluku and Sadiku's joy at seeing the one she held dear like a son.

'Nwaluku will stay with me until the time is right. As for you, my dear, you have to return home and pretend as if nothing has happened until I tell you what to do.'

I nodded silently.

Towards dawn, Nwaluku accompanied me towards the Abiyosa plantation. When we were close, he paused and drew me into his arms.

'My love, the gods have favoured us. I could not be here if you had not kept me alive with your love and faith in the healer. The time has come for us to avenge Sidi, to avenge the torment that Abiyosa has put you and Grandmother through, and above all, to avenge all the wrongdoings he had done to everyone. We will have to be patient. You know he is a very cunning man and we have to tread carefully,' he said, holding me by the shoulders.

'Yes, Lwuku. It is high time we make him pay for all his sins,' I said, my once-lost mojo back.

We hugged tightly as lost lovers could and parted ways. My Lwuku was back and it was time to give the old fox a very huge dose of his own medicine. It was time to go for the kill.

CHAPTER TWENTY-FIVE

Mornings had never looked this beautiful, neither did the sound of the morning birds caress my ears with such tenderness. I sat up amid my array of mats, my mind at ease. Events of the previous night had surely sent a boost of energy through my body. My strength was renewed, my fire ablaze and my heart pumped like the thunder of the heavens. Nwaluku was alive and kicking. I still was in disbelief about what I had witnessed and I so wished that Sidi was with me. We could be chatting away at this very moment; joy shared between us, yet my confidant was gone forever. Tears rolled down my cheeks, falling on my naked belly. The pain of many nights just poured out. Nwaluku was back, but no one could fill up the void that I felt. Deep were the scars that her death had left in my heart. Deep was the crevice that even Nwaluku's love could not fill up. Wiping off my tears, I dressed and got ready to face my new day, my new life.

The cool breeze hit my face as I stepped out of the hut. Sadiku was sitting by her fireplace, enjoying the heat on her now weary skin. I approached her hut gingerly like a cat stalking a lizard. I didn't know how I was to break the news to her, but I had to do so without scaring her. She had become so fragile so I had to be careful with how I laid out this big news to her. If Sidi had been here, she would have blurted the news out and sent the old lady into a coma.

'Is it time to have your ever so famous sour porridge, Granny,' I asked drawing a bench that the boys had discarded recklessly.

'It is you, child. Oh, that little one better come out as a strong boy or my sour delicacy would have gone to waste,' she said, with a voice filled with motherly love.

I had come a long way with this old woman. To think that she had made my first days in this place miserable, but now she was the only mother that I knew and loved dearly.

'Not at all, Granny. Now that your grandson is ready to come out, I have to eat a lot so that he won't look like a skinny mosquito.'

'Hehehe, this child? Have you ever seen a fat mosquito in your life?' she chuckled, as she scooped out spoonful after spoonful of sour porridge.

She handed me the bowl after adding a little sugar and a pinch of herbs, to make me strong and energetic during child birth, so she said.

'Granny I have something important to tell you.'

'Speak away, child, I am listening.'

I cleared my throat, but before I could utter a word my darling aunt graced us with her presence.

'There you are, you witches! Still planning my down fall?'

Aunt Paulina's distinctive voice echoed above ours.

'Now what do you want? You know it's still very early for human beings to deal with wild animals like you. Shouldn't you be in bed at this time trying to warm that wasted engine of yours,' I shot back at her my fury building up.

After what I had been through the night before, I had renewed energy such that my huge belly would not stop me from panel beating the one woman who was a prickling thorn in my backside.

'Child, do not waste your breath on her. Women like her aint worth the time,' Sadiku said.

'I was not talking to you, fishbones! I'm here to talk to this wretched witch; this child who has not only stolen Abiyosa from me, but has taken my peace of mind.'

I stared at Aunt Paulina and my blood began to boil. All I could see was a barrier and reason for all the pain that I had suffered. Without warning I lifted the steaming bowl of porridge and threw it straight into her face.

'Ohh mayee, this child! This child wants to kill me. Somebody, help me,' Aunt Paulina screamed, taking off her upper clothes.

Sadiku sprang from her place and emptied a bucket of water on her.

'Thando! Thandolwethu! If you want to kill me at this old age, please just feed me poison,' Sadiku shouted at me, shaking me like a river reed.

The help hands that worked in the plantation had gathered and were ogling the half-naked, half-drenched and half-porridge-coated Paulina. Some snuffled laughs as they dared not laugh out loud in case they face her wrath. The ruckus brought Abiyosa out of his hut and he came to assess the situation.

'What is all this? What is all this noise about,' he barked like a male baboon fighting potential mates off his female.

Wistfully, I knelt in front of him and in my ever sweet and apologetic voice I spoke.

'Husband, I'm very sorry. I did not realise aunt was coming my way. Accidentally, I tripped and the bowl of porridge flew out of my hand and happened to find a landing space on her chest,' I said, my big brown eyes swelling with tears.

'Liar! Liar! You wanted to kill me. This pregnant thing wanted to kill me, darling. Sort her out now,' Aunt Paulina shouted.

Abiyosa walked towards her and examined her burns.

'Aww love, these are just minor burns. The porridge just burnt you through your clothes. It's nothing serious, but the way you were screaming was like a spear had pierced your heart.'

'It's more like it has. Why are you not concerned about what this idiot has done to me?' she screamed.

'If you were dead I would be concerned, but you not, so stop the drama. You are embarrassing yourself,' Abiyosa said in his dismissive voice.

The gleam of anger and frustration that clouded Aunt Paulina's face was worth the hide of a cow. I turned to her.

'Aunt, forgive my clumsiness. It was a mistake. I'm very sorry. I didn't mean to trip and throw hot scalding porridge on you. Please forgive me.'

'There! You see? Your sister wife is apologising for her mistake. Now stop acting immature and get dressed. You are drawing unnecessary attention to yourself,' Abiyosa said, turning on his heels and heading back to his dwellings.

The mini crowd that had gathered to view the drama dispersed. When only Sadiku, Paulina and I were alone, I spoke.

'*Nsazo kunyisa uzwile*!,' I said, getting on my feet as I had been kneeling to show respect and remorse in front of Abiyosa. (*I'm yet to trouble you, understand!*)

'You... '

'Stop! If I were you, I wouldn't even dare to open that hole under your nose'.

I halted her insults. She gaped like a fish out of water, but words failed her. Turning on her heel, she left for her hut.

'*Nci, nci, nci*. Thando, my child. Heeh!' Sadiku said, beating the palms of her hands together.

I went over to her and hugged her tightly.

'I'm sorry, Grandmother, but I can't stand anyone insulting my mother-in-law. No, I can't. Nwaluku won't be happy to hear that you are being treated like this,' I said cupping her wrinkled face in my hands.

'I know, child. Oh may his soul rest in peace. My son taken away from me. Oh! *Umhlaba lo*,' she said, shaking her head sadly.

'What if your son could come back to you, Grandmother? What if your Nwaluku could return?'

168

'Hush, child. Those gone to the land of the dead never return, but only remain as our spiritual guides.'

'Nwaluku is alive,' I said quietly, stroking her cheek.

Her old weary eyes widened in fear as she searched to see if this was one of my many practical jokes I was fond of pulling on her.

'Child, this joke is not funny at all. Never joke about the dead this way,' she said her voice heavy with sadness.

'No. Grandmother, this is not a joke. Follow me,' I said dragging the old lady to her feet. It was time to reunite mother and son.

We trundled down the bush path deep into the overgrown brush. Sadiku kept on trying to coax me to tell her where I was taking her and why I had said her son was alive. Brushing this old woman off was a huge task. The walk to the edge of the village was not an easy one. With Sadiku's weary legs it took us longer than we had anticipated such that by mid-morning we were saluting and announcing our presence at a yard that looked like a fortress for dead animals. Every space had carcasses of various animals and the air in the yard smelled foul of burning herbs. We waded our way through the forest of carcasses until we got to the huge hut that stood at the far corner of the yard. Out of nowhere a big dog came charging at us, barking madly its teeth drooling with saliva. I let out a scream and clutched Sadiku's arm.

'*Futsek! Futsek! Shuuu!*,' Sadiku shouted at the dog that kept on coming close and snapping at our feet.

'For a person who is not afraid of the dark, you surely a sport to watch at this moment,' the sangoma's voice said as a log whizzed past my ankles and sent the dog whining away after it connected with its back. I chuckled shyly. The old man was right. I could brave the dark and a lot of things, but I was super scared of dogs.

The healer led us to his big hut and offered us warm tea. That was one thing that always baffled me about people in this area. No matter what the time of day a visitor approached, instead of offering any other refreshment, tea was always on the menu. As we sipped the hot tea, I took note of the hut we were in. The walls were decked with all the regalia of a sangoma, animal skins, snake skins, and all types of different carcasses. The floor was laden with skins of different types of animals. If you looked at them for a long time, you would swear they were moving.

'Mother, I called you here because I need you to meet someone,' the sangoma broke the silence. Sadiku stared blankly at him, her expression unreadable.

'Some moons ago, I came across a young man on the brink of death. He was barely alive when I found him, but I knew my ancestors had led me to him for the aura surrounding was of a strong force. He was unconscious and had suffered many severe wounds. With the gift that the gods bestowed on me, I managed to get him back to health and helped him embrace his calling. Your daughter here was the only link missing in bringing him back, and when she managed to perform the ritual for him, despite being heavy with child, your son was brought back to us'.

'No! Impossible. I saw his shredded clothes. I saw them drenched in blood and I mourned him like any other mother would. Who are you to tell me that my Nwaluku is alive? Are you working for that witch who has made our lives miserable?'

'No, Grandmother. The healer is telling the truth. Please do not attack the poor old man now.'

Nwaluku's voice thundered over the shrill wail of Sadiku's.

Sadiku's face turned deathly pale as she stared at the huge figure who was blocking the entrance to the hut. Time seemed to stand still as mother and son locked eyes like two bulls at a rodeo. Time came to a halt as untold and unexpressed emotions emitted energy only a mother and son could understand.

'My child, my Nwaluku,' Sadiku sobbed, tears of joy creating rivulets on her wrinkled face.

'Grandmother, Grandmother,' Nwaluku said, in a wavering voice that cut through my heart. I couldn't control my own river of tears as I watched this reunion. The sangoma sniffed his tears away.

'Are you crying, Makhosi?' I whispered to him teasingly.

'What me? Stop talking nonsense or I will put a curse on you,' he said pointing his staff at me.

'Now you believe me, Grandmother? Now you believe me and all my feelings,' I sobbed happily.

'You never lost your hope, Thando child. As long you had not yet seen his body, you believed he would come back. I'm sorry, my son. Your poor old Grandmother didn't have the same hope as Thando.'

'Grandmother, all will be put in place. All will be the way it's supposed to be. It is time, Grandmother. It is time for us to take back the lives that Abiyosa took away from us. And now that the ancestors have blessed me with this gift, I will not leave a stone unturned in punishing this scoundrel,' Nwaluku said, his voice full of hate.

We all nodded in unison. Abiyosa's time to face the music had come.

After our return from meeting Nwaluku, Sadiku's health changed. There was a certain spring to her step and she didn't seem so bothered by any of Aunt Paulina's taunts. Neither did she care about how she bossed everyone around her. Even the cats and dogs scurried away at the sight of Paulina.

I was now very heavy with child and any day I was ready to pop. Time was passing rapidly and phase one of my revenge plot was now ready to be intensified.

Aunt Paulina had a habit of wondering off to visit some friends of hers and come home late every Friday, but on this day she was to get what was coming to her. What I had in store for her was going to be beyond her wildest nightmares. I lay restlessly on my mat waiting for Sadiku to doze off. She had improved in such a way that with the spring in her step came a little bit of flesh on her bones. When I heard her deep snores start to shake the roaches off the rafters, I crept out of the hut to meet Nwaluku. It was a dark night with a few scattered fluffy clouds hanging lazily. Nwaluku was a sight of splendour. Clad in his sangoma regalia, I hardly recognised him as the young man I had so fallen in love with. We made our way to Aunt Paulina's hut and lay in wait for her.

After what seemed like hours, I heard her distinct humming as she was coming through the gate. Due to the many problems she was having with Abiyosa, she had taken to the cannabis drink so much that every night she would go and spend whatever money she salvaged from Abiyosa's pocket. She sashayed like a swan with a broken leg and got into her hut, bumping into whatever was in her way.

'Oh damn it!' she cursed, kicking over a pot I had placed in her way. I stifled a laugh. Fumbling in the dark, she found the box of matches and lit a candle. The eerie glow of the room filled the hut with shadows and I cowered at the end of the bed out of aunt's sight. Nwaluku was the one to do the honours of teaching this old hag a lesson.

'Hello, aunt, miss me?' he asked as he stepped from behind the door.

'You! No. You. No. This is a dream. You are not real,' Aunt Paulina said as she turned to come face to face with Nwaluku. It was not just plain Nwaluku, but the sangoma clad one.

'Yes, aunt. It's me. I'm back. Did you think you would get rid of me this easily?'

'No! You are dead. You are a spirit. I go to church and you can never touch me. Fire! Holy Fire,' Paulina cried throwing pillows at Nwaluku.

'*Nci, nci, nci.* Not even your fire or your holy spirit will spare you today. Every dog has its day, aunt, and yours has come today,' he said, advancing menacingly towards her.

It took all my will power not to burst into shrieks of laughter.

'Get back, Satan! Oh, my humble gods please save me. The Devil is tempting me,' my aunt sobbed hysterically.

'Shhh! Old woman. No one can hear you and if you keep on screaming and shouting you will drive me crazy. You will make me do things unimaginable to you. Maybe I should start with that fine behind of yours. I really need to make a powerful spell with it,' Nwaluku growled at her.

'Please son, please, my son, spare me. It's that Abiyosa who… '.

'Shut up! Enough! The time to pay for your sins has come. Prepare to meet your ancestors,' Nwaluku said drawing the huge knife that hung from his waist.

They say fear is one of the many weaknesses that tends to overcome humans. Aunt Paulina might have been a tough bully, but deep within she was just a scared little girl. Without warning, she let loose of her bowels and everything just came out freely. The stink that hit my nose even sent my unborn baby kicking up a storm. Damn! The old lady had messed herself!

'Please, my child. Spare me, child. I will never do it again,' aunt begged for her miserable life dropping to her knees and sobbing hysterically. Nwaluku blew out the candle and the hut plunged into darkness. As if on cue, I made my way through the dark hut towards the door. As I passed my aunt, I couldn't resist giving her a hard kick which sent her wailing.

We quickly made our way out of the hut. Nwaluku led me back to my hut and left for his dwelling before the dawn caught up with him. I kindled the ambers and set the fire ablaze. Daybreak was an hour away and I was sending Aunt

Paulina packing, not just packing, but to the same place she sent my Sidi. It was time she met her maker!

CHAPTER TWENTY-SIX

Daybreak not only brought joy to my heart, but also brought about the chance I had been waiting for to take my revenge on my dear, ever so loving, aunt. If the night's events had not shaken her then she was bound to get what was coming to her on this very day. Despite being heavily pregnant and ready to pop, I was bent on avenging Sidi's death.

Shouts and screams from aunt's hut made me hastily rush to the main kitchen to see what the commotion was all about. Aunt Paulina was beside herself with fear. She was throwing her belongings aimlessly into bags, eager to get out of the compound as fast as she could. Everyone in the yard was watching perplexed at this unfolding drama.

'Paulina, what is wrong, my love? Why are you acting so strangely?' Abiyosa asked, his voice an epitome of worry. Oh, poor man. If only he knew I was responsible for his lovely mistress's mad rant.

'I'm not staying one second in this place. I am leaving you Abiyosa. This yard is cursed and haunted by the ghost of that wretched boy Nwaluku.'

'What are you talking about? You see I've told you many a times to lay off the cannabis drink, but that thick head of yours wouldn't take any heed. Now look at what you are doing, acting all crazy.'

'I am not crazy. I'm not. I saw him last night. He wanted to kill me, Abiyosa. Oh God! Why did you have to kill the boy, Abiyosa? Now I am paying for your sins,' Paulina blurted out, dragging her two bags behind her.

Abiyosa's face turned ashen and he choked on his words.

'What are you talking about, Paulina? I think you have a massive hangover. That's why you are talking nonsense.'

'Enough, Abiyosa! Last night I almost died because of your sins. You killed Nwaluku and now he is haunting me. Now he wants to kill me for your sins. Enough mister! I'm not going to pay for deeds that I am not responsible for,' Aunt Paulina said at the top of her voice.

A sounding slap sent her sprawling to the ground. The monster I had wanted to awaken had decided to get out of hibernation without any effort from me. Abiyosa's mouth was frothing at its corners. He looked like a mad dog with rabies.

'Shut up! Shut up this very instant. I will kill you, Paulina. Stop talking nonsense.'

'Kill me, Abiyosa. Kill me now. Just as you killed Nwaluku, just as you killed Sidi. Go ahead. I would rather die than have a ghost haunt me.'

Oh! Poor aunt. She had just cemented her lover's fate by her confession. I walked over to her and put my arms around her.

'Don't worry, aunt. I will make sure you die a slow painful death just like you did my Lwuku, just like you sent Sidi to her death. *Khona uzonya,* aunt,' I whispered to her. (*You're yet to suffer, aunt*)

She let out a yell of anguish as a group of women led her to her hut. Her massive drama had attracted a crowd as usual and now the villagers were starting to murmur about all that Paulina had been blabbering. With both their deaths mysterious, Aunt Paulina's rant had sent tongues wagging. As the crowd dispersed, Abiyosa angrily got into his truck and drove away. He was a big fish I needed an inferno to cook.

Aunt Paulina's state turned from bad to worse. She dared not go to sleep on her own. As days went by, the women who had been kind enough to spend the nights in her hut soon gave up, as 'the ghost' tormented Paulina and the women until they packed their bags and left for their homes. She tried to reel in Sadiku, but she turned a deaf ear. Aunt Paulina was now on her own with no one to help her. Abiyosa began to be a scarce commodity following the cat that aunt had let out of the sack. Rumours circulated around the night fires as everyone had their own version of what was going on at the Abiyosa compound.

As for yours truly, I did not give rat's ass about what was happening and to whom. I had suffered a lot at these people's hands such that my heart had turned super stone cold. Anyone who saw aunt would swear she was being eaten by some deadly fungi from within. Her once full blossom began to sag and her velvet skin began to look as if a tsunami had hit her. Everyone in the village began calling her the mad woman Paupau, as she was seeing ghosts that no one could see. Nwaluku kept up his midnight hauntings and finally drove her to insanity.

It was one a fine morning that a wail broke the dawn for everyone. It was not just a normal wail, but one filled with sorrow and pain. Everyone rushed out of their huts, neighbours made their way towards our compound in masses. I woke up Sadiku and we hurried towards the huge crowd that had gathered outside the yard under the acacia tree, the same acacia tree on which Sidi took her last breath. Abiyosa was on his knees and beside himself with grief. Hanging from the very same branch that my dear sister had hung from some years ago was Aunt Paulina. Her now stiff body hung like a rag discarded by the winds. Out of guilt and fear of the unknown, Aunt Paulina could not withstand the terror that she succumbed to every night. There was one easy way out for her. Suicide!

Oh karma! Just as Sidi could not face her humiliation and pain, Aunt Paulina couldn't face her crimes and had taken the easy way out of her peril. She had hanged herself to end her misery.

Abiyosa was torn beyond measure. He sobbed and wailed like a small child with a broken toy and I couldn't care less. Everyone had their eyes on me, ready to see if I was going to take up the task of mourning for aunt. Well, they had another think coming. When requested to perform the final rites for her, I gladly denied and pointed to her grief stricken husband. Abiyosa buried Aunt Paulina on his own. None of the villagers even dared to help him dig the grave for her and none turned up for fear of the ghost that had sent her to death. Abiyosa buried his mistress on his own as people watched from afar. A pang of pity did cloud my heart for a second, but memories of Sidi immediately dismissed it. I was rid of the woman who had taken away my childhood, taken away my family and life. Next up was my dear loving husband, Abiyosa.

Aunt Paulina's death came as a huge blow on Abiyosa. It hit him hard from within and his world came crashing down. Despite the fact that he had caused me a lot of pain, I somewhat felt pity for him. He became so withdrawn from everything that mattered to him. His life turned into a mournful sight and that was what I wanted to see, him broken and helpless. He turned to the cannabis drink and found solace for a few moments, but whenever he was sober his nightmares came back.

'Thandolwethu! You are a curse to my life. I curse the day I ever set my eyes on you,' he said one day after he had had one too many. As usual I ignored him because they say you have to fatten the cow before slaughter.

'A curse you say, dear husband? You haven't seen a curse in your life. Your mistress was just the start, darling,' I retorted.

'Spare me. Please go away from here. Leave my life. Don't ever come back. I beg you, go.'

Listening to him plead gave me a kick that I could not explain and I so wanted to get out of the horrid place and return home, home to my long lost family.

That noon I found myself pushing my bulgy stomach as I headed towards the field where Sidi had been buried. My time in this place was done for and before I could leave I needed to pay my last respects to the girl who had been my family. Sidi's grave lay under a tree that always cast a shade over it. I always thought that it was a good spot for at least she wouldn't worry about getting sunburnt.

'My beloved sister, my pillar of strength. I'm leaving at day break, Sidi. I wish I could take you with me. I wish you could be here to share in my victory. You left me all alone, left my unborn child with no aunt and made me an orphan. I've avenged your death *sthandwa sami*, but only half of it. I need to finish what I started. Then your death will be avenged. Tonight I will avenge all the pain we went through and all the hardships,' I said, crying my eyes out beside her grave. Warm arms came around me and I turned to find Nwaluku and Sadiku beside me.

'Enough child, enough now. You don't have to stress the baby. You still have one task before you and you need to be strong. Enough now.'

Sadiku's soothing motherly voice managed to pacify me.

'Thando, my love all is ready for us to leave. Only you have to do what you are destined to do. End this evil once and for all,' Nwaluku said looking deeply into my eyes.

'Won't you be with me, Lwuku? What if I can't do it?'

'No, dear. This is a task meant only for you. You have your fulfill your destiny. This is what was written in your stars at your birth. You have to do this,' he said reassuringly.

Yes. I had to do as per my destiny. I had to finish this bad chapter of my life, break the curse so that it won't follow my child; break the chain.

Night fell quickly for me and my nerves began to get the better of me. I paced like a caged lion until Sadiku complained that I was making her dizzy. I couldn't help it at all. I had packed and repacked my bags repeatedly trying to pass time. Abiyosa was in his hut, hiding from the world as he still was mourning the death of the love of his life. He had reduced to what the locals would call a zombie for he was more like the walking dead. No one seemed to care for the plantation and the few loyal workers were helping themselves to whatever they could salvage.

I walked slowly to Abiyosa's hut, my fear enveloping me like a blanket. The night was pitch black as if the heavens sensed that something was about to go down. The stars caressed the dark sky and the moon shone. His door was ajar so I let myself into the dimly lit room.

'What do you want? Haven't you done enough? Be gone, Satan. Be gone from my life, Thando. You are definitely a curse to me,' he shouted.

'Every dog has its day, husband and your day has come,' I said, striking him hard on his head with a spade. He reeled over and fell from the stool he was sitting on.

'So now you will attack me, Thando? No pain you can inflict on me will ever be the same as the one I am feeling now. I have lost everything. My beloved is dead thanks to you, so what more can you do to me?'

'Your beloved, you say? You took my life away from me; you raped me, Abiyosa. You took my family away from me and the future that lay bright before me. So, mister, you have no right to cry over losing that witch. She deserved what she got just like you deserve what is happening to you,' I said, emptying a bucket of petrol on him.

With the help of one of the tractor drivers at the plantation, we had drained dry one of Abiyosa's cars. My heart stopped beating for a while as I watched the man who had made my life a living hell look so helpless. He looked at me with eyes filled with fear.

'What is this? You ... ' he said, trying to get up.

He met with another wham from the spade I had. That sent him crashing to the floor. I turned on my heels and left the hut, bolting the door from the outside. Walking to the kitchen, I came back with a flaming log. My hands shook uncontrollably. I felt no remorse but just bottled up emotions. Through the glow of the log I could see Sidi's lifeless body, her cold eyes staring at the heavens as if begging for mercy. My anger was fueled even more. With all my might, I tossed the log through the window at the human heap that was still struggling to get on its feet. With a whoosh, flames engulfed the man who had turned me from a bubbly, innocent girl to a vengeful monster. Agony-filled screams broke through the night as the fire spread out through the hut and sent a huge blaze casting long shadows. I turned away from the burning hut and walked without a backward glance. I climbed into the truck that was waiting for me, Nwaluku and Sadiku beside me.

'It is done, child. Let us go,' Sadiku said, urging the driver to pull away. As the truck trundled down the dusty road, the glare from the burning hut lighting the way, I looked back once more at the compound that had been my prison for years and tears rolled down my cheeks. I had won; I had conquered.

A rose smells sweet. A rose is a symbol of love. A rose is woman with thorns that prick only those who handle her carelessly. Be a rose. Be sweet. Be full of love, but never forget how sharp your thorns are.

Thorns of a Rose

Thorns of a Rose